ESSENTIAL SPANISH

Nicole Irving & Leslie Colvin
Illustrated by Ann Johns
Designed by Adrienne Kern

Additional designs by Brian Robertson

Language consultants: Graciel·la Edo de Grigg
& Marión Lorente Moltó

Series editor: Gaby Waters

Contents

About this book

This phrase book will help you to survive, travel and socialize. It supplies simple, up-to-date Spanish for holidays and exchange visits. It also gives basic information about Spain and tips for low budget travellers.

The language is everyday, spoken Spanish. This can differ from textbook Spanish and ranges from the correct to the colloquial, and from the polite to the casual, depending on the region, the situation and the person speaking.

Use the Contents list to find the section you need or look up words in the Index. Remember that you can make yourself clear with words that are not quite right or with very few words. Saying *"¿Valencia?"* while pointing at a train will provoke *sí* or *no* (yes or no). Words like *por favor* (excuse me) or *gracias* (thank you) make anything sound more polite and generally guarantee a friendly response. For anyone who is

ready to have a go, the Spanish listed below is absolutely essential.

●Newcomers to Spanish should look through Spanish pronunciation and How Spanish works (pages 50-53).

●Words are given in the form likely to be most useful. The level of politeness is pitched to suit each situation and casual *tú* and *vosotros/as* forms or polite *usted* and *ustedes* forms are given as appropriate. If in doubt, use the polite form.

●An asterisk after a Spanish word shows it is slang or familiar, e.g. is good-looking *está bueno/buena**.

●(m) is short for masculine, and (f) for feminine.

●Adjectives with two forms are given twice: masculine/feminine, e.g. red *rojo/roja*.

Absolute essentials

Do you speak English?	*¿Habla inglés?*[1]	1 *uno*	11 *once*
	¿Hablas inglés?[2]	2 *dos*	12 *doce*
I don't understand.	*No entiendo.*	3 *tres*	13 *trece*
Can you write it down?	*¿Puede escribirlo?*[1]	4 *cuatro*	14 *catorce*
	¿Puedes escribirlo?[2]	5 *cinco*	15 *quince*
Can you say that again?	*¿Puede repetir?*[1]	6 *seis*	16 *dieciséis*
	¿Puedes repetir?[2]	7 *siete*	17 *diecisiete*
A bit slower, please.	*Un poco más despacio, por favor.*	8 *ocho*	18 *dieciocho*
What does this word mean?	*¿Qué significa esta palabra?*	9 *nueve*	19 *diecinueve*
What's the Spanish for this?	*¿Cómo se dice esto en español?*	10 *diez*	20 *veinte*

yes	*sí*	see you, bye	*hasta la vista*	when?	*¿cuándo?*
no	*no*	see you later	*hasta luego*	where?	*¿dónde?*
maybe	*quizás*	see you soon	*hasta pronto*	why?	*¿por qué?*
I don't know.	*No lo sé.*	see you	*hasta*	because	*porque*
I don't mind.	*No me importa.*	tomorrow	*mañana*	how?	*¿cómo?*
please	*por favor*	good morning	*buenos días*	how much?	*¿cuánto?*
thank you	*gracias*	good evening	*buenas tardes*	How much is	*¿Cuánto*
not at all	*de nada*	good night	*buenas noches*	it?	*cuesta?*
sorry	*perdone*[1]	How are	*¿Qué tal?*	What is it/this?	*¿Qué es esto?*
	perdona[2]	things?		it is	*es*
excuse me	*perdone*[1]			this is	*esto es*
	perdona[2]	Mr, Sir	*señor*[3]	is there?	*¿hay?*
I'm very	*me sabe muy*	Mrs, Madam	*señora*[3]	there is	*hay*
sorry	*mal*	Miss	*señorita*[3]	I'd like	*quisiera*[1]
hello, hi	*hola*				*quiero*[2]
goodbye, bye	*adiós*	and	*y*		
		or	*o*		

[1]Polite form. See page 51. [2]Familiar form. See page 51. [3]In Spanish these are often used on their own, without a name. See page 12.

Asking the way

Fact file

You will find an *Oficina de Información y Turismo* (tourist office) in most big towns and cities, often near the station or town hall. In tourist areas even small towns have one. Opening times are usually 9-1 and 3.30-6 on weekdays and 9-1 on Saturday. In small places, opening times may be restricted.

Most tourist offices provide town plans and leaflets on local sights free of charge. They also give advice on places to stay and travel arrangements. They often employ someone who speaks English. Some tourist offices sell maps and specialist booklets on local footpaths, wildlife etc., although these may be in Spanish.

Directions

It's on the left/right.	*Está a la izquierda/ derecha.*
Go left/right.	*Vaya a la izquierda/ derecha.*
Go straight ahead.	*Vaya todo recto.*
Take the first on the left.	*Tome la primera a la izquierda.*
Take the second turning on the right.	*Tome la segunda bocacalle a la derecha.*
Follow the signs for Cadiz.	*Siga las señales para Cádiz.*
It's...	*Está...*
Go...	*Vaya...*
Carry on...	*Siga...*
straight ahead	*todo recto*
Turn...	*Gire..., Tuerza...*
left	*izquierda*
right	*derecha*
Take...	*Tome...*
the first	*la primera*
the second	*la segunda*
the third	*la tercera*
the fourth	*la cuarta*
turning	*la bocacalle*
on the left	*a la izquierda*
on the right	*a la derecha*
crossroads, junction	*el cruce de carreteras*
roundabout	*el cruce giratorio*
traffic lights	*el semáforo*
pedestrian crossing	*el paso para peatones*
subway	*el paso subterráneo*
Cross...	*Cruce...*
Follow...	*Siga...*
street	*la calle*
road	*la carretera*

main...	... principal
alley	el callejón
path	la senda, el camino
(main) square	la plaza (mayor)
motorway	la autopista
ringroad	la carretera de circunvalación
one way	dirección única
no entry	dirección prohibida
dead end	calle sin salida
no parking	prohibido aparcar
car park	el aparcamiento
parking meters	los parquímetros
pedestrian area	la zona peatonal
pedestrians	los peatones
pavement	la calzada
town centre	el centro de la ciudad
area, part of town	el barrio
outskirts, suburbs	las afueras
town hall	el ayuntamiento
bridge	el puente
river	el río
railway line	la vía del tren
post office	la oficina de correos
shops	las tiendas
church	la iglesia
school	el colegio, la escuela
cinema	el cine
museum	el museo
park	el parque
just before the	justo antes de
just after the	justo después de
at the end	al final
on the corner	en la esquina
next to	al lado de
opposite	en frente de
in front of	delante de
behind	detrás
above	encima, por encima
beneath	abajo
over	sobre
under	debajo
in	en, dentro
on	en, encima
here	aquí
there	allí
over there	por allí
far	lejos
close, near	cerca
nearby, near here	cerca de aquí
around here	por aquí
somewhere	en alguna parte
in this area	en esta zona
10 minutes walk	diez minutos a pie
5 minutes drive	cinco minutos en coche
by bike	en bicicleta
on foot	a pie

¿Cómo se va al camping?
What's the best way to the campsite?

¿Puede indicármelo en el mapa?
Can you show me on the map?

¿Dónde está la playa más cercana?
Where's the nearest beach?

¿Queda muy lejos?
Is it far?

¿Por dónde se va a el albergue juvenil?
How do I get to the youth hostel?

Travel: trains, underground, buses

Getting information

What time is the next train to Madrid?

How long is the journey?

Do I have to change?

Tickets

Where can I buy a ticket?

How does this machine work?

Can I have a single to Granada?

Finding the right bus

Where does the bus for Valencia leave from?

Is this the right bus for Barcelona?

Can you tell me where to get off?

¿Dónde tengo que transbordar para ir a el Retiro?

¿De qué andén sale el tren para Sol?

¿Qué acaban de decir por el altavoz?

| Where do I change for el Retiro? | What did they just say over the loudspeaker? | Which platform for Sol? |

¿Hacen algún tipo de descuento?

Can I get a reduction?

Fact file

For getting around Spain, *autobuses interurbanos* (long-distance buses) are a good option as they are frequent, cheap and go to remote places. There are many bus companies and buses to the same destination may leave from different places. For information, try the tourist office, bus station or, in a small place, a bar. Get tickets at the bus station or on the bus.

RENFE (Spanish railways) runs a complicated train service. The standard trains are *Expreso* and *Rápido*. *Talgo*, *Ter* and *Electrotrén* are faster and more pricey. Buy tickets in advance to save later confusion over which supplements you have to pay. Fares are cheaper on off-peak *días azules* (blue days). There are a few private railway companies — details from tourist offices.

Some cities have a *metro*, but they all have *autobuses urbanos* (city buses). Ten ticket booklets, e.g. *Bono-bus*, work out cheaper — available from *estancos* (tobacconists). There's little public transport on Sundays.

railway station	la estación de tren	book of tickets	un taco de billetes
underground station	la estación de metro	student fare	la tarifa de estudiante
bus station	la estación de autobuses	youth fare	la tarifa joven
bus stop	la parada de autobús	supplement	el suplemento
train	el tren	I'd like to reserve a seat.	Me gustaría reservar un asiento
underground train	el metro		
tram	el tranvía	left luggage locker	la consigna automática
bus, coach	el autobús	map	un mapa
leaves at 2[1]	sale a las dos	timetable	un horario
arrives at 4.30	llega a las cuatro y media	arrivals	llegadas
first	primero/primera	departures	salidas
last	último/última	long distance	largo recorrido
next	próximo/próxima	local, suburban	cercanías
cheapest	más barato/barata	every day, daily	diario
ticket office	la taquilla de billetes, la ventanilla	weekdays[2] (including Saturdays)	laborables
		Sundays and holidays	domingos y festivos
fare	el precio, la tarifa	in the summer-time	en verano
ticket	un billete...	out of season	fuera de temporada
single	...de ida	except	excepto
return	...de ida y vuelta		

[1]For times, see page 54. [2]For days of the week, see page 54.

Travel: air, sea, road

Air and sea

I'd like to confirm my flight.

What time should I get there?

Where do I check my bags in?

My luggage hasn't arrived.

Mrs Serra is supposed to be meeting me.

Fact file

Airports and harbours often have signs and announcements in English. There's usually a bus or train from the airport into town — generally the cheapest option.

Taxis are cheap with metered fares, but it's wise to ask what the fare will be first. Taxis usually take up to four passengers. They charge extra at night, on Sundays and for large bags.

A...
Take me to...
¿Cuanto costaria ir a...?
What's the fare to...?
Pare aqui, por favor.
Please drop me here.

airport	*el aeropuerto*	information	*información*
port	*el puerto*	customs	*la aduana*
aeroplane	*el avión*	visa	*el visado*
ferry	*el barco*	passport	*el pasaporte*
flight	*vuelo*	departure gate	*la puerta de salida*
(sea) crossing	*travesía*	boarding pass	*la tarjeta de embarque*
Mediterranean	*Mediterráneo*	ferry ticket	*un billete de barco*
Atlantic	*Atlántico*	No smoking	*No fumador*
rough	*bravo, picado*	travel agent	*una agencia de viajes*
calm	*liso, en calma*	airline ticket	*un billete de avión*
I feel sea sick.	*Estoy mareado / mareada.*	cut price	*de precio reducido*
		standby	*aviso*
on board	*a bordo*	charter flight	*un vuelo charter*
to check in	*facturar*	package holiday	*unas vacaciones organizadas*
suitcase	*la maleta*		
backpack, rucksack	*la mochila*	flight number	*el número de vuelo*
bag	*una bolsa*	a booking	*una reserva*
hand luggage	*el equipaje de mano*	to change	*cambiar*
heavy	*pesado / pesada*	to cancel	*cancelar*
trolley	*el carrito*	a delay	*un retraso*

On the road

Tengo una avería.

¿Dónde esta el taller mas cercano?

I've broken down.   Where's the nearest garage?

No sé por qué no funciona.

I don't know what's wrong.

¿Puede repararlo usted?

Los frenos no funcionan.

Can you fix it?   The brakes don't work.

Fact file

Bikes and mopeds are often available for hire in tourist areas. You can ride a moped from age 14 but make sure you are insured. It's illegal not to wear a crash helmet even though many people ignore this.

Remember the Spanish drive on the right. Drivers should always carry a valid driving licence. Theft from cars is a problem in some areas, so keep documents with you and your things out of sight.

toll[1]	*peaje*	motorbike	*una moto*
insurance	*el seguro*	crash helmet	*un casco*
driving licence	*el carnet de conducir*	battery	*la batería*
(car) documents	*los papeles*	jump leads	*cables para la batería*
petrol station	*una gasolinera*	spark plugs	*las bujías*
petrol	*la gasolina*	fan belt	*el ventilador*
lead-free petrol	*gasolina sin plomo*	radiator	*el radiador*
oil/petrol mixture	*mezcla de aceite y gasolina*	gears	*las marchas*
		to hitch[3]	*hacer autostop*
		lights	*las luces*
oil	*el aceite*	chain	*la cadena*
litre	*un litro*	wheel	*la rueda*
car	*un coche*	cable	*el cable*
moped	*una motocicleta*	brakes	*los frenos*
		pump	*un compresor de aire*
bicycle[2]	*una bicicleta*	tyre	*el neumático*
bike	*una bici*	inner tube	*la camara*

garage, repair shop	*un taller*
I have a puncture.	*Tengo un pinchazo.*
Fill it up, please.	*Lleno, por favor.*
The engine won't start.	*El motor no arranca.*
The battery's flat.	*La batería esta descargada.*
How much will it cost?	*¿Cuanto costara?*
Can I hire...?	*¿Alquilan...?*
for hire	*de alquiler*

Travel talk

¿Adónde vas?
Where are you going?

Voy a Cadiz.
I'm going to Cadiz.

¿Has estado en Sevilla?
Have you been to Seville?

¿Como es?
What's it like?

[1]There is a toll on some Spanish motorways. [2]See page 41 for different kinds of bikes. [3]It's not advisable to hitch.

Accommodation: places to stay

At the Tourist office

Do you have a list of campsites?	I'm looking for a room for two people.	Can you book a room for me?

Hotels

Do you have a room?	We're full.	Is there another hotel nearby?

Fact file

The *Oficina de Información y Turismo* (tourist office) will supply lists of places to stay. Cheap accommodation includes: *fondas* – rooms, often above a bar; *casas de huespedes* – guest houses; *pensiones* – rooms, price may include food; *hostales* – cheap hotels. The word *residencia* means no meals are served except breakfast. You might also see signs for *camas* (beds), *habitaciones* (rooms) and *camas y comidas* (beds and meals) advertised in private houses or above bars. Sharing a room is always cheaper. *Campings* (campsites) vary in price and quality, and can be crowded in summer. *Albergues de juventud* (youth hostels) are basic and rarely the best option, except in the north.

Camping

Do you have a space?

Rooms to let	habitaciones	Can I have my passport back?	¿Puede devolverme el pasaporte?
How much do you want to pay?	¿Cuánto quieres pagar?		
How many nights?	¿Cuántas noches?	tent	una tienda
One/two night(s).	Una/dos noche(s).	caravan	una caravana
single room	una habitación individual	restaurant	un restaurante
		swimming pool	una piscina
double room	una habitación doble	hot water	agua caliente
room with 3 beds	una habitación triple	cold water	agua fría
clean	limpio/limpia	drinking water	agua potable
cheap	barato/barata	camping gas	camping gas
expensive	caro/cara	guy rope	un viento
lunch	la comida	tent rings	las arandelas
dinner (evening)	la cena	tent peg	una estaquilla
full board	pensión completa	mallet	un mazo
half board	media pensión	torch	una linterna
key	la llave	box of matches	una caja de cerillas
room number	el número de la habitación	loo paper	el papel higiénico
		can opener	un abrelatas

¿Cuánto cuesta una habitación?

How much for a room?

¿El precio incluye el desayuno?

¿Puedo ver la habitación?

Does that include breakfast?   Can I see the room?

Somos tres personas con una tienda.

¿Tienen algún comercio?

¿Es potable el agua del grifo?

¿Dónde podemos ir a nadar?

There are three of us with a tent.   Do you have a shop?   Is it OK to drink the tap water?   Where can we swim?

Accommodation: staying with people

Greetings

¡Hola!
Hello.

¿Cómo estás?
How are you?

For more polite or formal greetings, use the expression most appropriate to the time of day followed by *Señor* or *Señora* (see page 3). Also use the polite form ¿*Cómo está?* (How are you?)

¿Dónde puedo dejar mis cosas?

¿Dónde tengo que dormir?

Where can I put my things?   Where am I sleeping?

¿A qué hora tomáis desayuno?[1]

¿Puedes despertarme a las siete?[2]

What time do you have breakfast?   Could you wake me up at seven?

Washing

¿Cómo funciona la ducha?

¿Puedo lavar algo de ropa?

How does your shower work?   Do you mind if I wash a few things?

Is it OK to have a bath?	¿Puedo tomar un baño?	bath	el baño
Can I borrow a towel?	¿Puedes prestarme una toalla?	shower	la ducha
		towel	una toalla
Where can I dry these?	¿Dónde puedo secar esto?	soap	jabón
		shampoo	el champú
		deodorant	el desodorante
		toothpaste	el dentrífico
bathroom	el cuarto de baño	hairdryer	el secador
loo, toilet	el lavabo, los servicios	washing powder	jabón en polvo

[1/2]To be polite, when speaking to a stranger or an older person, say [1]¿A qué hora toman desayuno? [2]¿Puede despertame a las siete?

Being polite

¿Puedo ayudar a pagar los gastos?

No te preocupes.

Can I pay my share?   No, don't worry.

Gracias por alojarme.

Si necesito algo ya lo pediré, gracias.

It's nice of you to let me stay.   I'll ask if I need anything, thanks.

Saying goodbye

Muchas gracias por todo.
Thank you for everything.

¡Adiós!
Goodbye.

Using the phone

¿Puedo llamar por teléfono?
Can I use your phone?

Pagaré la llamada.
I'll pay for the call.

¿Cuánto cuesta llamar a Gran Bretaña?
How much is it to call Britain?

See page 15 for more about phones and making phone calls.

I'm tired.	Estoy cansado/cansada.
I'm really exhausted.	Estoy muerto/muerta de cansancio.
I'm cold.	Tengo frío.
I'm hot.	Tengo calor.
I'm fine.	Estoy bien.
Can I have a key?	¿Puedo tener una llave de la casa?
What is there to do in the evenings?	¿Qué se puede hacer por las noches aquí?
Where's the nearest phone box?	¿Dónde está la cabina más próxima?
alarm clock	un despertador
sleeping bag	un saco de dormir
on the floor	en el suelo
blanket	una manta
sheet	una sábana
pillow	una almohada
electric socket, plug	un enchufe
needle	una aguja
thread	el hilo
scissors	unas tijeras
iron	una plancha
upstairs	arriba
downstairs	abajo
cupboard	un armario
bedroom	el dormitorio
living room	la sala de estar
kitchen	la cocina
garden	el jardín
terrace, balcony	la terraza

Banks, post offices, phones

Banks

I want to change this.

Do you accept Eurocheques?

Can I see your passport?

Money problems

I've lost my traveller's cheques.

The serial numbers were...

How do I get replacements?

Phones[1]

This phone doesn't work.

Is this the code for Barcelona?

Hello, is María there please?

[1]For more phrases on using the phone see page 13.

bank	*el banco*	by airmail	*por avión*
cashier's desk, till	*la caja*	a stamp for	*un sello para*
foreign exchange	*extranjero, cambio*	Britain	*Gran Bretaña*
enquiries	*información*	the USA	*Estados Unidos*
money	*el dinero*	Australia[2]	*Australia*
small change	*la calderilla*	registered letter	*una carta certificada*
traveller's cheques	*unos cheques de viaje*	poste restante	*lista de correos*
credit card	*una tarjeta de crédito*		
exchange rate	*la tarifa de cambio*	telephone office	*Telefónica, la oficina*
commission	*la comisión*		*de teléfonos*
a (money) transfer	*una transferencia*	telephone	*un teléfono*
from Britain	*desde Gran Bretaña*	telephone box	*una cabina de teléfono*
		directory	*un listín telefónico,*
post office	*Correos, la oficina de*		*una guía de teléfonos*
	Correos	phone number	*el número de teléfono*
postcard	*una postal*	wrong number	*el número equivocado*
letter	*una carta*	reverse charge call	*una llamada a cobro*
parcel	*un paquete*		*revertido*
envelope	*un sobre*	Hang on.	*Un momento.*

Estoy esperando un envío de dinero, ¿ha llegado?

I'm expecting some money, has it arrived?

Post offices

¿Me dá un sello para esta carta?

Can I have a stamp for this letter?

¿Dónde está el buzón más cercano?

Where's the nearest postbox?

¿Cuándo volverá?
When will she be back?

¿Puedo dejar un recado para...?
Can I leave a message for...?

Por favor, dígale que he llamado.

¿Podría decirle que me llame?
Can she/he call me back?

Please tell her/him I called.

Mi número es...
My number is...

Fact file

The unit of currency is the *peseta (Pta)*. The 5 *pesetas* coin is called a *duro*. Banks open 8.30-2 on weekdays, 9-1 on Saturday (not always in summer). You can change money elsewhere (look for the sign *cambio*) but you may get a poorer exchange rate. There's a good system of cashpoints. Some take foreign cashpoint cards.

Phone boxes take coins. For international calls, look for the sign *Teléfono Internacional*. You can also phone from bars, department stores or a *Telefónica*. These phones are metered and you pay after the call. For useful phone numbers see page 47.

You can buy stamps in a post office or an *estanco* (tobacconist, see page 22).

[2]For names of other countries see page 55.

Cafés

café	el café
bar	el bar
table	una mesa
chair	una silla
at the bar	en la barra
Cheers!	¡Salud!
something to drink	algo de beber
something to eat	algo de comer
black coffee	un café solo
white coffee	un café con leche
lemon tea	un té con limón
tea with milk	un té con leche
hot chocolate	un chocolate caliente
fruit juice	un zumo de fruta
orange juice	un zumo de naranja
coke	una coca-cola
mineral water	un agua mineral
still	sin gas
fizzy	con gas
bottle of beer	una botella de cerveza
glass of draught beer	una caña
glass of red wine	un vaso de vino tinto
half a bottle of white wine	media botella de vino blanco
milk	la leche
sugar	el azúcar
with ice	con hielo
slice of lemon	una rodaja de limón
olives	unas aceitunas
cheese roll	un bocadillo de queso
cheese sandwich	un sandwich de queso
ham (cooked)	jamón de York
ham (cured)	jamón serrano
ice-cream	un helado

Fact file

There is little difference between Spanish bars, cafés and *cafeterías*. They are good for drinks, snacks, meeting friends or using the loo and phone. Most cafés open 9.30 am to 11 pm. Prices vary (smart means pricey). If you sit down, a waiter serves you but everything is cheaper at the bar. Go to *una granja* for afternoon drinks and pastries.

Try *café con hielo* (strong black coffee to which you add sugar and ice) or *zumo de naranja natural* (freshly squeezed orange juice). Look out for *tapas* (starter like dishes), see page 19. Other snacks: *churros* (doughnuts), omelettes (*española* has potato, *francesa* is plain) and sandwiches.

¿Vamos a tomar un café?
How about a cup of coffee?

¿Está ocupada esta silla?
Is this chair taken?

¿Puedo ver el menú?
Can I see the menu?

Un café solo, por favor.
A black coffee, please.

¿Tienen batidos?
Do you have milkshakes?

17

Eating out[1]

Choosing a place

¿Dónde vamos?

No me gustan las pizzas.

Vamos a comer una hamburguesa.

Where shall we go?   I don't like pizzas.   Let's go for a hamburger.

Spanish food	la comida española	chips	patatas fritas
Italian ...	... italiana	sausages	unas salchichas
Chinese ...	... china	fried egg	huevo frito
cheap restaurant	un restaurante barato	salad	una ensalada
(food) to take away	para llevar	spaghetti	unos espaguetis
menu	el menú	steak	un bistec
starter	el primer plato	rare	muy poco hecho/ hecha
main course	el segundo plato		
dessert	el postre	medium	poco hecho
price	el precio	well done	muy hecho
soup	la sopa	mustard	la mostaza
fish	el pescado	salt	la sal
meat	la carne	pepper	la pimienta
vegetables	las verduras	dressing	la vinagreta
cheese	el queso	mayonnaise	la mayonesa
fruit	la fruta		
		Are you enjoying it?	¿Te gusta?
hamburger	una hamburguesa	Yes, it's very good.	Sí, está muy bueno.

Problems

La carne está poco hecha.

Yo pedí una paella.

¿No tienen salsa de tomate?

I ordered *paella*.   The meat isn't cooked enough.   Don't you have any ketchup?

[1]There are also food words on pages 16, 21 and 25.

Deciding what to have

¿Qué es eso?

Tomaré uno de esos.

¿Puede hacer uno sin queso?

What's that?	I'll have one of those.	Can I have one without cheese?

Fact file

Spanish food is worth exploring and good value but to eat out cheaply you need to be adventurous – there aren't many fast-food places.

Look out for bars that serve *tapas* (snacks or starter like dishes). These include olives, *chorizo* (spicy salami) seafood such as *gambas* (prawns) or *calamares* (squid), *habas* (beans), etc. The dishes are often on the counter so you can point to show what you want. Have one *ración* (portion) as a snack or several as a meal. Alternatively order *unos platos* (a large plateful). *Tapas* are cheap but remember that in most bars, prices are even lower if you eat at the counter.

There are lots of restaurants serving good, inexpensive food. Try *un restaurante* or, for local food, *una fonda*. Most of these display a *menú turístico* (set menu) with its price. This is usually three courses with a drink and is often good value. *El menú del día* (dish of the day) or the *platos combinados* (various dishes served on one plate) can both be cheap.

Most bills say *Servicio incluido* (service included) but tipping is normal practice so it's best to leave a small tip.

Meal times are late. Lunch begins at 1, 2 or 3 and dinner after 9. It can be cheaper to buy your own food (see page 25).

¡Por favor!

Excuse me!

¿Puede traernos la cuenta, por favor?

Can we have the bill please?

Yo no había pedido eso.

I didn't order this.

Helping

Can I help?

Can I lay the table?

Can I do the washing-up?

He comido bastante, gracias.
I've had enough thanks.

La comida estaba muy buena.
That was delicious.

breakfast	*el desayuno*	tuna fish	*el atún*
lunch	*la comida, el almuerzo*	hake	*la merluza*
		monkfish	*el rape*
dinner	*la cena*		
glass	*el vaso*	pasta	*la pasta*
plate	*el plato*	rice	*el arroz*
knife	*un cuchillo*	potatoes	*las patatas*
fork	*un tenedor*	onions	*las cebollas*
spoon	*una cuchara*	garlic	*el ajo*
		carrots	*las zanahorias*
bread	*el pan*	peas	*los guisantes*
jam	*la mermelada*	spinach	*las espinacas*
butter	*la mantequilla*	aubergine	*la berenjena*
margarine	*la margarina*	asparagus	*los espárragos*
		artichokes	*las alcachofas*
chicken	*un pollo*	tomatoes	*los tomates*
pork	*la carne de cerdo*	cucumber	*el pepino*
		red/green pepper	*el pimiento rojo/verde*
beef	*la carne de vaca*		
veal	*la carne de ternera*	raw	*crudo/cruda*
		(too) hot/spicy	*(demasiado) picante*
liver	*el hígado*		
		salty	*salado/salada*
squid	*el calamar*	sweet	*dulce*
prawns	*las gambas*		

Enjoy your meal.	*¡Buen provecho!*
I'm thirsty/hungry.	*Tengo sed/hambre.*
I'm not hungry.	*No tengo hambre.*

Fact file

Breakfast is coffee with pastries or toast. Mid-morning snacks are common. The main meal is at about 3 and it is often three courses. Soups may be cold. Water, wine and bread are always served and pudding is often fruit. The evening meal is lighter and late, at 9, 10 or even 11.

Special cases

No me gusta el pescado.

I don't like fish.

Soy vegetariano [1].

I'm a vegetarian.

Soy alérgico [2] a los huevos.

I'm allergic to eggs.

There aren't many vegetarians in Spain, so be ready to explain. If you're a girl, say *vegetariana*. If you're a girl, say *alérgica*.

Shopping

Can I help you?   I'd like one of these.

How much is this?   523 pesetas.

Please write that down.   That's fine.   I'll take it.

Shops

main shopping area	el centro comercial
department store	unos grandes almacenes
market	el mercado
supermarket	un super, supermercado
shop	una tienda
general shop, grocer	una tienda (de comestibles), un colmado [1]
baker	una panadería
cake shop	una pastelería
butcher	una carnicería
delicatessen	una charcutería
fruit/veg stall, greengrocer	una verdulería
fishmonger	una pescadería
health food shop	una tienda naturista, herboristería
hardware shop	una ferretería
chemist	una farmacia
chemist (non-dispensing)	una droguería
camera shop	una tienda de fotografía
jeweller	una joyería
gift department	objetos de regalo
tobacconist	un estanco
news kiosk	un quiosco de periódicos
stationer	una papelería
bookshop	una librería
record shop	una tienda de discos
flea market	un rastro
sports shop	una tienda de deportes
shoe shop	una zapatería
shoe mender	un zapatero
hairdresser	una peluquería
barber	un barbero
laundry [2]	una lavandería
travel agent	una agencia de viajes
open	abierto/abierta
closed	cerrado/cerrada
entrance	la entrada
exit	la salida
check-out	la caja
lift	un ascensor
stairs	una escalera
price	el precio

[1]The word *colmado* is used in Catalonia. [2]These can be cheap. There are few launderettes except in tourist areas. Some campsites have washing machines.

Fact file

Opening times vary but bear in mind that shops close for lunch. Shops generally open Monday to Friday 9.30 to 1.30 and 4 or 5 to 7.30 or 8, and 9.30 to 2 on Saturday. Many bakers are also open on Sunday morning. Department stores open 10 to 8 without a break, Monday to Saturday. Look out for the sign *cerrado los* (closed on ...).[3]

An *estanco* sells stamps as well as cigarettes. A *ferretería* sells handy things for camping but try a *tienda de deportes* for camping equipment. A *farmacia* has medicines and plasters and a *perfumería* sells make-up, shampoo, soap etc. but things like this are cheaper in department stores, e.g. *el Corte Inglés*.

The best and cheapest place for food and everyday things is a *tienda de comestibles*. They can be small but they sell everything including wine, meat, fruit and vegetables. Some sell bread but each village has at least one *panadería*. There are few greengrocers. People buy their fruit and vegetables from a *tienda* or a market.

Markets are held regularly. Big towns have them daily and smaller places twice a week. They're colourful and lively as well as being good for food and local produce.

For picnic things, go to a *tienda* or buy sandwiches from a *tapas* bar (see page 19). In cities you might find a *charcutería* where you can buy sausages, salamis, ham etc.

Finding the right place

Where's the main shopping area?

Do you sell batteries?

Where can I get batteries?

Where can I get this repaired?

Where's a good place for sunglasses?

Necesito una crema bronceadora.

I need some sun-tan lotion.

¿Tienen una más grande?

Is there a bigger one?

English	Spanish	English	Spanish	English	Spanish
sunscreen[1]	una crema con protección total	aspirin	unas aspirinas	sunglasses	unas gafas de sol
make-up	el maquillaje	plasters	unas tiritas	jewellery	las joyas
(hair) gel	el gel fijador	film	una película	watch	un reloj
mousse	el mousse	English newspapers	unos periódicos ingleses	earrings	unos pendientes
tampons	unos tampones	postcard	una postal	ring	un anillo
tissues	unos pañuelos de papel	writing paper	el papel de escribir	purse	un monedero
razor	una maquinilla de afeitar	envelope	un sobre	bag	una bolsa
shaving foam	espuma de afeitar	notepad	una libreta	smaller	más pequeño/ pequeña
contact lens solution	la solución para las lentes de contacto	ball-point pen	un bolígrafo	cheaper	más barato/ barata
		poster	un poster	another colour	otro color
		badges	unas insignias		
		stickers	unos adhesivos		

¿Qué desea?

De momento, sólo quiero mirar.

Can I help you?   I'm just looking.

¿Puedo ver ése?

Can I see that one?

¿Cuánto cuesta?

How much is it?

Quiero pensarlo un poco.

I want to think about it.

Food shopping [3]

Quisiera dos panecillos.

I'd like two rolls.

¿Puede darme setenta pesetas de uvas?

Can I have 70 pesetas worth of grapes?

¿Puede darme un poco de ese pâté?

Can I have a bit of that pâté?

¿Así?

Un poco más, por favor.

Like that?

A bit more please.

Vale, así está bien, gracias.

Ok, that's enough thanks.

carrier-bag	una bolsa	peanuts	unos cacahuetes
small	pequeño/pequeña		
large	grande	fruit	la fruta
a slice of (meat)	una tajada	apples	manzanas
a bit more	un poco más	pears	peras
a bit less	un poco menos	bananas	plátanos
a portion	una porción	oranges	naranjas
a piece of	un trozo de	grapefruit	pomelos
a kilogram	un kilo	mandarins	mandarinas
half a kilo	medio kilo	peaches	melocotones
100 grammes	cien gramos	nectarines	nectarinas
		plums	ciruelas
bread [2]	el pan	figs	higos
stick	una barra	strawberries	fresas
round loaf	una hogaza	cherries	cerezas
wholemeal bread	pan integral	apricots	albaricoques
savoury pie	una empanada	dates	dátiles
sweets	unos dulces	blackberries	moras
chocolate	el chocolate	melon	un melón
crisps	unas patatas	watermelon	una sandía
	fritas, unas papas	pineapple	una piña

[2] A standard loaf is *una barra*. If you want something smaller, ask for *una barra pequeña*. [3] See pages 16-21 for more food words.

Can I try this on?   Do you have it in a small?   I need a bigger size.

That looks awful.   Does this look OK?   It looks fine.   It doesn't suit me.

The zip's broken.   I've just split my jeans.   Where did you get those?

¿Lo tienen en otro color?

Do you have this in another colour?[1]

Necesito un imperdible.

Could I have a safety pin?

clothes	la ropa	tights	unas medias
shirt	una camisa	socks	unos calcetines
T-shirt	una camiseta	swimsuit, trunks	un bañador
sweatshirt, jumper	un jersey	hat	un sombrero
dress	un vestido	cap	una gorra
(mini)skirt	una (mini) falda	small	pequeño/ pequeña
jean skirt	una falda vaquera	medium	mediano/ mediana
trousers	unos pantalones	large	grande
jeans	unos vaqueros, unos tejanos	extra large	extra grande
		too big	demasiado grande
shorts	unos pantalones cortos	smaller	más pequeño/ pequeña
tracksuit	un chandal	long	largo/larga
trainers	unas zapatillas de deporte	short	corto/corta
		tight	ceñido/ceñida
		baggy	suelto/suelta
		fashion	la moda
shoes	unos zapatos	a look, style	un estilo
sandals	unas sandalias	fashionable	de moda
boots	unas botas	trendy, cool	chulo/chula
cowboy boots	unas botas camperas	out-of-date, untrendy	pasado de moda
braces	unos tirantes	smart	elegante
belt	un cinturón	dressy	bien vestido/ vestida
(ski) jacket	un anorak		
boxer shorts	unos calzoncillos	scruffy	desastrado/ desastrada
bra	un sostén	sale	las rebajas
pants	unas bragas	changing room	el probador

¿Puedes prestarme tu chaqueta?

¿Llevo el traje de baño?

¿Puedo ir en tejanos?

Are jeans all right?

Can I borrow your jacket?

Shall I bring my swimming stuff?

[1]See page 54 for a list of colours.

Music

¿Dónde hay una buena tienda de discos?

Where's a good place to buy records?

¿Tienen una sección de jazz?

¿Tienen esto en casete?

Do you have a jazz section?   Do you have this on cassette?

Types of music

This list includes music you're likely to hear in Spain. For other types of music, try using the English word as the names are often the same.

heavy metal	*heavy metal*
hard rock	*rock duro*
rock	*rock*
alternative	*música alternativa*
punk	*punk*
reggae	*reggae*
soul	*soul*
rock & roll	*rock & roll*
jazz	*jazz*
blues	*blues*
folk	*folk*
flamenco	*flamenco*
afro-cuban	*música afro-cubana*
Brazilian	*música brasileña*
salsa	*salsa*
pop	*pop*
dance/disco	*disco*
slow dances	*lentos*
classical	*clásica*

Can I put some music on?	¿Puedo poner música?
I've never heard any...	Nunca he oído...
I listen to (lots of)...	Escucho (mucho)...
Turn it up.	Sube el volumen.
It's too loud.	Está demasiado alto.
Turn it down.	Baja el volumen.
Can you tape this record for me?	¿Puedes grabarme este disco?
music	la música
record shop	una tienda de discos
radio	la radio
radio-cassette player	un radio-casete
record-player	un tocadiscos
hi-fi	una cadena de alta fidelidad
Walkman †, personal stereo	un Walkman, un stereo personal
headphones	unos auriculares
(radio) station	una emisora
single	un single, un sencillo
album	un elepé
compact disc	un compact disc
blank tape	un casete virgen
music video, pop video	un video musical, un video-pop
song, track	una canción

¿Qué tipo de música te gusta?

¡Son malísimos!

What kind of music do you like?

They're useless.

†A Walkman is a Sony product.

¿De quién es?

¿Has visto el video?

Who's this by?

Have you seen the video?

¿Puedes prestarme este elepé?

Can I borrow this album?

lyrics	la letra
tune, melody	una melodía
rhythm	el ritmo
live music	música en directo
group, band	un grupo
solo artist	un solista
singer	el cantante
singer-song writer	un canta-autor
lead vocalist	el vocalista
accompaniment, backup	el acompaña-miento
fan	un/una fan
member of the group	un miembro del grupo
tour	una gira
concert, gig	un concierto
benefit concert	un concierto benéfico
the Top 40[1]	los cuarenta principales
number one	el número uno
hit	un éxito
latest	último/última
new	nuevo/nueva
50's music	música de los cincuenta

Playing an instrument

Do you play an instrument?	¿Tocas algún instrumento?
I play the guitar.	Toco la guitarra.
I'm learning the drums.	Estoy aprendiendo a tocar la batería.
I play in a band.	Toco en un grupo.
I sing in a band.	Canto en un grupo.

instrument	un instrumento
piano	el piano
keyboards	el teclado
drum machine	la caja de ritmos
electric guitar	la guitarra eléctrica
bass guitar	la guitarra baja
saxophone	el saxofón
trumpet	la trompeta
harmonica	la armónica
violin	el violín
flute	la flauta
choir	un coro
orchestra	una orquesta

¿Has oído su último disco?

¡Es fantástico!

Have you heard the latest album?

It's brilliant.

[1] The most common pop chart in Spain is the Top 40.

Going out: making arrangements, sightseeing

Making arrangements

What's happening? Have you got any ideas?

Shall we do something tonight?   I can't, I'm busy.

Do you know a good place to...	¿Sabes de un buen sitio para...
go dancing?	ir a bailar?
listen to music?	escuchar música?
eat?	comer?
go for a drink?	ir de copas?
nightclub, club	un club nocturno, una disco
disco	una discoteca
party	una fiesta
picnic	un picnic, una excursión
barbecue	una barbacoa
show, entertainment	un espectáculo
cinema	un cine
ballet	ballet
opera	opera
in town	en el centro
at X's place	en casa de X
on the beach	en la playa

Can I get a ticket in advance?	¿Puedo comprar una entrada por adelantado?
ticket office	la taquilla
student ticket	una entrada de estudiante
performance, film showing	una sesión
What time does it...	¿A qué hora...
start?[2]	empieza?
finish?	acaba?
open	abierto/abierta
closed	cerrado/cerrada
today	hoy
tonight	esta noche
tomorrow	mañana
day after tomorrow	pasado mañana
morning	la mañana
afternoon	la tarde
evening	la noche
this week	esta semana
next week	la semana que viene

Sightseeing

What is there to see around here?	¿Qué se puede ver por aquí?
guide book	una guía
things to see	los lugares a visitar
tour	una excursión
region	la región
area	la zona
countryside	el campo
mountains	la montaña
lake	el lago
river	el río
coast	la costa
museum	un museo

art gallery	una galería de arte
exhibition	una exposición
craft exhibition	una exposición de artesanía
the old town	el centro histórico
city walls	las murallas
cathedral	la catedral
church	una iglesia
mosque	una mezquita
castle	un castillo
tower	una torre
statue	una estatua
monument	un monumento
ruins	unas ruinas

caves	unas cuevas
safari park	el safari park
theme park	el parque de atracciones
water park	el parque acuático
festival	el festival
fair	la feria
bullfight	una corrida de toros
fireworks	los fuegos artificiales
interesting	interesante
dull, boring	aburrido/aburrida
beautiful	bonito/bonita

[1]Say *Estoy ocupada* if you're a girl. [2]See page 54 for days, dates and time.

¿Dónde nos encontramos?

¿A qué hora?

Where shall we meet?   What time?

Nos vemos en la fuente.

See you at the fountain.

Deciding what to do

¿Qué quieres hacer?

¿Vamos a una disco?

¿Quién toca en el Jazz Bar?

What do you want to do?   Let's go to a nightclub.   Who's playing at the Jazz Bar?

¿Dan alguna película buena?

¿Hay algo interesante?

No quiero hacer nada.

What's on?   Are there any good films on?   I don't want to do anything.

Fact file

If you want to find out what to visit, go to the tourist office (see page 4). Here you will get free maps, town plans and leaflets.

To find out what's on, look at the back pages of local newspapers. Most cities have listings magazines and towns have *carteleras* (billboards). Many films are dubbed but some are in *version original* (original language) or *vo*. People go out late. The last film showing is at 10.30 or 11. Clubs may not fill up until 1 am.

Films, TV, books etc.

Films and TV

Books, magazines etc.

cinema	un cine	award-winning	ganador/a de un premio
film soc/club	un club de cine	block buster	la película taquillera
theatre	un teatro	a classic	un clásico
library	una biblioteca	comedy	una comedia
film, movie	una película	thriller	una película policíaca
play	una obra de teatro		
book	un libro	musical	un musical
magazine	una revista	horror film	una película de terror
comic	un comic	adventure story	una historia de aventuras
novel	una novela		
poetry	poesía	war film	una película de guerra
author	el autor		
director	el director	a western	una película del oeste
cast	el reparto		
actor/actress	el actor/actriz	sci-fi	ciencia ficción
film buff	un experto en cine	suspense	suspense
production	una producción	sex	sexo
plot	el argumento	violence	violencia
story	la historia	political	político/política
set	el decorado	satirical	satírico/satírica
special-effects	los efectos especiales	serious	serio/seria
photography	la fotografía	offbeat	original
TV	la televisión	fringe	marginal
telly	la tele	commercial	comercial
satellite TV	la televisión satélite	exciting	emocionante
late-night TV	la televisión de madrugada	a tear jerker	un drama
		over the top	exagerado/exagerada
programme	el programa		
channel	el canal	good	bueno/buena
news	las noticias	OK	bien
documentary	el documental	bad	malo/mala
soap	el serial	lousy	malísimo/malísima
ads	los anuncios		
dubbed	doblado/doblada	silly	tonto/tonta
in English	en inglés	funny, fun	divertido/a
with subtitles	con subtítulos	sad	triste
famous	famoso/famosa	scary	de miedo

33

Talking about yourself

Where are you from?   I'm English.

What about you?

Where do you live?   I live near York.

How long have you been here?

What are you doing in Spain?

What do you think of Spain?

Where are you staying?

¿Cómo te llamas?

Jo.

What's your name? Jo.

¿Cuántos años tienes?

Tengo diecisiete.

How old are you? I'm seventeen.

¿Estás sola?

No, estoy viajando con amigos.

Are you alone? No, I'm travelling with friends.

¿Tienes alguna hermana?

Have you got any sisters?

I'm English.[1]	Soy inglés/inglesa.
My family is from...[1]	Mi familia es de...
I've been here for two weeks.	Hace dos semanas que estoy aquí.
I'm on an exchange.	He venido en un intercambio.
I'm on holiday.	He venido de vacaciones.
I'm staying with friends.	Estoy en casa de amigos.
I'm studying Spanish.	Estoy estudiando el español.
I'm travelling around.	Estoy viajando por el país.
I live...	Vivo...
in the country	en el campo
in a town	en una ciudad
in a house	en una casa
in a flat	en un piso
I live with...	Vivo con...

I don't live with...	No vivo con...
my/your	mi, mis[2]/tu, tus[2]
family	la familia
father/mother	el padre/la madre
husband/wife	el marido/la esposa
boyfriend/girlfriend	el novio/la novia
brother	el hermano
sister	la hermana
alone	solo/sola
single	soltero/soltera
married	casado/casada
My parents are divorced.	Mis padres están divorciados.
My name is ...	Me llamo...
nickname	apodo
surname	apellido
my address	mi dirección
My birthday is on the...[3]	Mi cumpleaños es el día...

[1]Words for nationalities, countries and religions are on page 55. [2]Use *mi* and *tu* with singular words, *mis* and *tus* with plural words. See page 52. [3]For days and dates, see page 54.

Other people

Gossip

Who's that?	Do you know Carlos?	What's happened to Paola?	What's she like?	We get on OK.

friend	un amigo/una amiga	is good-looking[1]	está bueno/buena *
mate, pal	un tío/una tía *	isn't good-looking[1]	no es guapo/guapa
boy/girl	un chico/una chica	is OK (looks)[1]	está bien
someone	alguien	ugly	feo/fea
has long hair	tiene el pelo largo	a bit, a little	un poco
short hair	el pelo corto	very	muy
curly hair	el pelo rizado	so	tan
straight hair	el pelo lacio	really	realmente
has brown eyes	tiene los ojos castaños	completely	completamente
he/she is...[1]	el/ella es ...	nice, OK	simpático/simpática
tall	alto/alta	horrible, nasty	horrible
short	bajo/baja	is trendy, right on[1]	está al día
fat	gordo/gorda	is old-fashioned, square[1]	está anticuado/anticuada
thin	delgado/delgada	clever	listo/lista
fair	rubio/rubia	thick	burro/burra
dark	moreno/morena	boring	aburrido/aburrida
pretty	guapa		

Making the first move

[1]There are two words for "is": es means "is (always)", e.g. Es alto (he is tall); está means "is (at the moment)", e.g. Está de mal humor (he is in a bad mood). You can often use either

He's a good laugh.	I like him.	He's tall.	I can't stand her.	She's quite pretty.

shy	timido/timida	a creep	un pelotillero/ una pelotillera
mad, crazy	loco/loca		
weird	raro/rara	an idiot	un/una idiota
lazy	vago/vaga	a prat	un/una gilipollas*
laid back	tranquilo/tranquila	in a bad mood	de mal humor
up-tight	tenso/tensa	in a good mood	de buen humor
mixed up, untogether	no se aclara	hassled, annoyed	enfadado/enfadada
selfish	egoísta	upset	preocupado/preocupada
jealous	celoso/celosa	depressed	deprimido/deprimida
rude	mal educado/educada	happy	feliz
macho	machista	Have you heard...?	¿Sabes qué...?
a bit smooth	un poco falso/falsa	Carlos is going out with Paola.	Carlos sale con Paola.
stuck up	pretencioso/ pretenciosa		
		Juan fancies Maria.	A Juan le gusta Maria.
sloaney	pijo/pija*	He/she kissed me.	Me besó.
yuppie	un/una yuppie	They split up.	Han roto.
cool	chulo/chula	We had a row.	Tuvimos una pelea.

to express different shades of meaning. However adjectives listed here with *está* should be used with this verb. See page 52.

No juego al squash.
I don't play squash.

Voy a correr cada mañana.
I go jogging every morning.

¡Rápido!
Quick!

¡Corre!
Run!

sport	un deporte	once a week	una vez a la semana
match	un partido		
game	una partida	twice a week	dos veces a la semana
doubles	dobles		
singles	individuales	I play...	Juego al...
race	una carrera	I don't play...	No juego al...
marathon	una carrera de maratón	tennis	tenis
		squash	squash
championships	unos campeonatos	badminton	badminton
		football	fútbol
Olympics	los Juegos Olímpicos	American football	fútbol americano
World cup	la Copa del mundo	basketball	baloncesto
		volleyball	balonvolea
club	un club	table tennis	tenis de mesa
team	un equipo	cricket	cricket
referee	un árbitro	baseball	béisbol
supporter	un/una hincha	I do/go...	Hago...
training	entrenamiento	I don't do/go...	No hago...
practice	práctica	judo	judo
a goal	un gol	karate	karate
to lose	perder	keep-fit	gimnasia (para estar en forma)
to draw	empatar		
sports centre	un centro de deportes		
		aerobics	aerobics
stadium	un estadio	weight-training	levantamiento de pesos
court	una pista		
indoor	cubierta		
outdoor	al aire libre	bowling	los bolos
ball	una pelota	dancing	baile
net	una red	I go jogging	voy a correr
trainers	unas zapatillas de deporte	I don't go running	no voy a correr
tracksuit	un chandal		

How do you play this?	¿Cómo se juega?
What are the rules?	Explícame las reglas del juego.
Throw it to me.	Tíramela.
Catch!	¡Cógela!
In!/Out!	¡Dentro!/¡Fuera!
You're cheating!	¡Haces trampas!
What team do you support?	¿De qué equipo eres?
Is there a match we could go to?	¿Podríamos ir a ver algún partido?
Who won?	¿Quién ganó?
What was the score?	¿Cuál fue el resultado?

Fact file

Spanish bull fighting is famous but it's not as popular as football. People play football, go to matches and watch it on TV, particularly in bars on Sunday evening. The big teams are *Real Madrid, F.C. Barcelona* and *Real Sociedad*. Tennis and basketball are popular. In the Basque country people play *pelota* (balls are hit against a wall with wicker rackets). There's an annual *Vuelta ciclista a España* (round Spain cycle race). Winter sports are becoming popular, with most resorts in the Pyrenees and the Sierra Nevada.

I like...	Me gusta...
I don't like...	No me gusta...
I love...	Me encanta...
I prefer...	Yo prefiero...
swimming	la natación
(scuba) diving	el submarinismo
sunbathing	tomar el sol
sailing	la navegación
surfing	hacer surf
water skiing	el esquí acuático
canoeing	el piragüismo
rowing	el remo
boat	una barca
surfboard	una plancha de surf
boom	la botavara
mast	el mástil
sail	la vela
sea	el mar
beach	la playa
pool	la piscina
in the sun	al sol
in the shade	a la sombra
goggles	las gafas de natación
mask	las gafas de submarinismo
snorkel	el tubo
flippers	las aletas
wetsuit	el traje de bucear
life jacket	un salvavidas
fishing	la pesca
rod	la caña

cycling	el ciclismo
racing bike	una bici de carreras
mountain bike	una bici todo terreno
touring bike	una bici de paseo
BMX	una bici BMX
horse riding	la equitación
horse	un caballo
walking, hiking	el excursionismo
skateboard	un monopatín
roller skating	el patinaje sobre ruedas
ice skating	el patinaje sobre hielo
ice rink	la pista de hielo
skates	los patines
skiing	el esquí
cross-country skiing	el esquí alpino
ski run	la pista
ski pass	el forfait
ski lifts	los remontes
chair lift	el telesilla
drag lift	el telearrastre, el telesquí
skis	los esquís
boots	las botas
bindings	las fijaciones
ski goggles	las gafas de esquí
snow	la nieve

| What do you do? | Where are you studying? | What sort of college is it? |

| What time do you finish? | Do you have a lot of work? | Yes loads. |

I'm a student.	*Soy estudiante.*	English	*inglés*
I'm still at school.	*Aún voy a la*	French	*francès*
	escuela.	German	*alemán*
		Italian	*italiano*
I'd like to do...	*Me gustaría hacer...*	Russian	*ruso*
I do...	*Estudio...*	Latin	*latín*
computing,	*informática*	Greek	*griego*
information		literature	*literatura*
technology		philosophy	*filosofía*
maths	*matemáticas, mates*	sociology	*sociología*
physics	*física*	religious studies	*religión*
chemistry	*química*	art	*arte*
biology	*biología*	art history	*historia del arte*
natural sciences	*ciencias naturales*	drama	*teatro*
geography	*geografía*	technical drawing	*dibujo técnico*
history	*historia*	PE	*educación física*
economics	*económicas*		
business studies	*estudios*	school	*un colegio, una escuela*
	empresariales	boarding school	*un internado*
politics	*ciencias políticas*	state education	*enseñanza pública*
languages	*idiomas*	private education	*enseñanza privada*
Spanish	*español*	term	*un trimestre*

Fact file: the Spanish system

Types of schools and colleges[1]:
—un colegio de enseñanza secundaria (first stage of secondary school — for all pupils aged about 12 to 15)
—un instituto de bachillerato (second stage, 16 to 18 — similar to sixth form college)
—una escuela de formación profesional (as above, but with technical, vocational slant)
—una universidad (university), split into various facultades (faculties).

School is compulsory until 16. State schools are mixed and there is no uniform. At each stage of secondary education the forms are called el primero, el segundo and el tercero[2]. There is continual assessment as well as a test for each subject every year. Anyone who fails has the option of retaking the test in September. At about 18 many pupils sit the Selectividad, the university entrance exam. Pupils have to travel to a university to sit this. El servicio militar (national service), also called la mili, is compulsory for men. The first call-up is at age 19 but it can be deferred for up to 15 years. A period of community service can be served instead.

during term time	durante el trimestre	continual assessment	evaluación continua
holidays	las vacaciones	mark, grade	nota
beginning of term	el principio del trimestre	teacher	el maestro/la maestra
uniform	un uniforme	lecturer	el profesor/la
club	un club		profesora
competition	un concurso	(language) assistant	ayudante de
lesson, lecture	una clase		conversación
tuition, private	clases particulares	good	bueno/buena
lessons		bad	malo/mala
conversation class	clase de conversación	easy going	tranquilo/tranquila
homework	deberes	strict	estricto/estricta
essay	un trabajo escrito	discipline	la disciplina
translation	una traducción	to repeat (a year)	repetir curso
project	un proyecto	to skive, to bunk off	hacer novillos, hacer
an option	una optativa		campana
revision	un repaso	to skip a lesson	saltarse una clase
test	un examen		
oral test	un examen oral	a grant	una beca
oral	oral	a loan	un préstamo
written	escrito	free	gratis
presentation	una exposición oral de un tema		

[1] The equivalents in brackets are only approximate. [2] Literally, these mean the first, second and third.

43

¿Qué tipo de actividades haces?
What sort of things do you do?

Trabajo en una tienda.
I work in a shop.

¿Tienes mucho tiempo libre?
Do you get a lot of spare time?

Me interesa mucho la fotografía.
I'm interested in photography.

Tengo una computadora personal.
I've got a PC.

¿Tienes algún juego?
Have you got any games?

¿Has jugado a Spider's Revenge?
Have you played Spider's Revenge?

¿A quién le toca?
Whose go is it?

¿Qué teclas tengo que tocar?
What keys do I have to press?

¿Qué hago ahora?
What do I do now?

I do a lot of sport.	Hago cantidad de deporte.
I listen to a lot of music.	Escucho muchísima música.
I write songs.	Escribo canciones.
I write poetry.	Escribo poesía.
I collect...	Colecciono...
all sorts of things	todo tipo de cosas
postcards	postales
matchboxes	cajas de cerillas
I like...	Me gusta...
drawing	dibujar
painting	pintar
knitting	hacer punto
making clothes	la coser
making jewellery	la joyería
yoga	el yoga
I work in a café.	Trabajo en una cafetería.
I do a paper round.	Reparto periódicos.
I do babysitting.	Trabajo de canguro.
a part-time job	un trabajo de jornada reducida
allowance	dinero de bolsillo

computer	una computadora	game	un juego
program	un programa	chess	el ajedrez
programming	programar	board games	juegos de tablero
word processing	procesador de datos	cards	las cartas
adventure game	juego de computadora	poker	el póquer
disk	un disco	easy	fácil
joystick	un mando	difficult	difícil
My go.	Me toca a mí.	What are the rules?	Puedes explicarme las reglas del juego?
Your go.	Te toca a ti.		

Plans

What do you want to do later?	¿Qué quieres hacer después?
When I finish...	Cuando acabe...
One day...	Un día...
I want...	Quiero...
to travel	viajar
to go to...[1]	ir a...
to live/work abroad	vivir/trabajar en el extranjero
to have a career	hacer carrera
to get a good job	obtener un buen trabajo
to get my qualifications	obtener las calificaciones necesarias
to carry on studying	continuar estudiando
I want to be a...	Quiero ser...
I don't want to be a...	No quiero ser...

> Quiero viajar alrededor del mundo.
> I want to go round the world.

> Yo tambien.
> So do I.

Issues

What do you think about...?	¿Qué piensas sobre...?	environment	el medio ambiente
I don't know much about...	No sé mucho sobre...	conservation	la conservación
		ecology	la ecología
Can you explain...?	¿Puedes explicar...?	ozone layer	la capa de ozono
I think...	Creo que...	animals	los animales
I believe in...	Creo en...	plants	las plantas
I'm for...	Estoy a favor de...	trees	los árboles
I support...	Soy partidario/a de...	deforestation	la desforestación
I belong to...	Soy de...	acid rain	la lluvia ácida
I don't believe in...	No creo en...	pollution	la polución
I'm against...	Estoy en contra de...	nuclear power	la energía nuclear
I feel angry about...	Me enfada que...	recycling	el reciclaje
I agree.	Estoy de acuerdo.	politics	la política
You're right.	Tienes razón.	government	el gobierno
I don't agree.	No estoy de acuerdo.	democratic	democrático/democrática
the future	el futuro		
(in) the past	el pasado	elections	las elecciones
now	ahora	party	el partido
important	importante	member of a party	un/una militante
		army	el ejército
		nationalism	el nacionalismo
religion	la religión	coup	un golpe de estado
god	dios	autonomous regions	las autonomías
human rights	los derechos humanos	the left	la izquierda
gay	gay	the right	la derecha
feminist	feminista	fascist	fascista
abortion	el aborto	communist	comunista
drugs	las drogas	socialist	socialista
drug addict	adicto	green movement, greens	los verdes
Aids	el Sida	conservative	conservador/conservadora
rich, well off	rico/rica		
poor	pobre	reactionary	reaccionario/reaccionaria
unemployment	el desempleo		
Third World	el Tercer Mundo	politically active, committed	políticamente activo/activa
peace	la paz		
nuclear disarmament	el desarmamento nuclear	a charity	una sociedad benéfica
war	la guerra	march, demonstration	una marcha, una manifestación

45

Illness, problems[1] and emergencies

doctor	un doctor, un médico
woman doctor	una doctora, una médica
dentist	un/una dentista
optician	un/una oculista, un óptico/una óptica
chemist[2]	una farmacia
pill[2]	una pastilla
suppository[3]	un supositorio
injection	una inyección
I'm allergic to...	Soy alérgico/alérgica a...
antibiotics	los antibióticos
some medicines	algunos medicamentos
I have...	Tengo...
food poisoning	una intoxicación
diarrhoea	diarrea
cramp	una rampa
sunstroke	una insolación
a headache	dolor de cabeza
a stomach ache	dolor de estómago
my period, period pains	el período, la regla*
an infection	una infección
a sore throat	dolor de garganta
a cold	un resfriado
hayfever	fiebre del heno
flu	una gripe
toothache	dolor de muelas
a temperature	fiebre
a hangover	una resaca
He/she's had too much to drink.	Ha bebido demasiado.
I feel dizzy.	Me siento mareado/mareada.
I'm constipated.	Tengo estreñimiento.
I've been stung by a wasp.	Me ha picado una avispa.
I've got mosquito bites.	Tengo picaduras de mosquito.
It hurts a lot.	Duele mucho.
It hurts a little.	Duele un poco.
I've cut myself.	Me he cortado.
I think I've broken my...	Creo que me he roto...
My ... hurts.	Me duele...
eye	el ojo
nose	la nariz
mouth	la boca
ear	el oído, la oreja
chest	el pecho
arm	el brazo
hand	la mano
wrist	la muñeca
finger	el dedo
leg	la pierna
knee	la rodilla
ankle	el tobillo
foot	el pie
bottom	el culo *
back	la espalda
skin	la piel
muscle	el músculo

No me encuentro bien.
I don't feel well.

¿Qué te pasa?
What's wrong?

Tengo ganas de vomitar.
I'm going to be sick.

Me sabe muy mal.
I'm really sorry about this.

Quiero ir al médico.
I need to see a doctor.

¿Hay alguna farmacia abierta por aquí?
Is there a chemist open around here?

¿Puede darme algo para la alergia?
Can you give me something for hayfever?

[1]For problems not listed here, try asking ¿Tiene un diccionario? (Do you have a dictionary?)
[2]Everyday things like plasters and aspirin are on page 24. [3]These are often prescribed in Spain.

Problems

He perdido una lente de contacto.
I've lost my contact lens.

Alguien ha robado mis cosas.
Someone's stolen my things.

Se me han roto las gafas.
I've broken my glasses.

No vi lo que pasó.
I didn't see what happened.

my wallet	*mi cartera*	There's no water/ power.	*No hay agua/corriente eléctrica.*
my handbag	*mi bolso*		
my things	*mis cosas*	I'm lost.	*Me he perdido.*
my papers	*mis papeles*	I'm in trouble.	*Tengo problemas.*
my passport	*mi pasaporte*	I'm scared.	*Tengo miedo.*
my key	*mi llave*	I need to talk to someone	*Necesito hablar con alguien.*
all my money	*todo mi dinero*		
lost property	*objetos perdidos*	I don't know what to do...	*No sé qué hacer...*
Can you keep an eye on my things?	*¿Puedes vigilar mis cosas?*	I don't want to cause trouble, but...	*No quiero molestar, pero...*
Has anyone seen...	*¿Alguien ha visto...?*	A man's following me.	*Un hombre me está siguiendo.*
Please don't smoke.	*Por favor, no fume.*		
Where's the socket?	*¿Dónde está el enchufe?*		
It doesn't work.	*¡No funciona!*		

Fact file

In Spain it's always advisable to carry proof of identity, so keep your passport with you. You may be asked to show your *papeles* (documents, ID). When carrying anything valuable or important, keep it out of sight.

For minor health problems or first aid treatment, go to a chemist. For something more serious go to a doctor. Look for an *Ambulatorio de la Seguridad Social* (local surgery). In an emergency go to a *Hospital de la Seguridad Social* (state-run hospital). In each case you should expect to pay. You should be able to claim back on insurance[4], but keep all the paperwork.

Watch out for these signs: *Prohibido el paso* (no entry); *Salida de emergencia* (emergency exit); *Peligro* (danger); *Propiedad privada* (private property); *Prohibido el baño* (no swimming); *Agua no potable* (not drinking water).

Emergencies

Emergency phone numbers: police, 091; ambulance and fire brigade, numbers vary. (From 1992, call 112 for all three services). For very serious problems contact the closest *Consulado Británico* (British Consulate). Find the number in the directory.

There's been an accident.	*Ha habido un accidente.*
Help!	*¡Ayuda!*
Fire!	*¡Fuego!*
Please call...	*Por favor, llame a...*
an ambulance	*una ambulancia*
the police	*la policía*
the fire brigade	*los bomberos*
the lifeguard	*el socorrista*
hospital	*un hospital*
casualty department	*emergencias*
police station	*la comisaría de policía*

---

[4] British passport holders can use an E111 form – available from the DSS.

Slang and everyday Spanish

¹If you're a girl, say *Déjame sola.* ²If you're a boy, say *Estoy harto.*

The Spanish that people use every day, especially amongst friends, is different in lots of ways from correct textbook Spanish. As in English, people use slang and have alternative ways of saying things. They also leave out bits of words (e.g. in English "I do not know" can end up sounding like "I dunno"). This book has included informal Spanish and slang words where appropriate, but these two pages list a few of the most common words and phrases.

When using colloquial language it is easy to sound off-hand or even rude without meaning to. This is especially true for slang words, so here as in the rest of the book an asterisk after a word shows it is mild slang and it is safest to experiment with it only amongst friends.

Contractions and alternative pronunciations

How are you?	¿Qué tal? (¿Qué tal estás?)
How are things?	¿Cómo va? (¿Cómo van las cosas?)
See you later.	Ta luego.* (Hasta luego.)
houses	casa* (casas)[1]
market	mercao* (mercado)[2]

Abbreviations

TV	la tele (televisión)
teacher	el profe* (el profesor)
disco, club	la disco (la discoteca)
mate, pal	el/la compa* (el compañero/la compañera)

American and English imports

un parking, un spot (a commercial, an ad), el look, sexy, stop, el estress (stress), el corner (in football), el club, el marketing, el heavy metal, el cassette or casete, el walkman, el estereo, el cheque...

Fillers and exclamations

OK	vale
you know	sabes
well	bien
...er...	bueno
then	luego, entonces
Really?	¿Ah, sí?
Hey!	¡Vaya!
Wow!	¡Caray!
by the way	por cierto
I mean, that's to say	o sea
(used to emphasize what follows, similar to American "man")	hombre, mujer
(means something is "so so" or OK)	psss
(shows you agree)	ya, ya

Slang

great, fantastic	(ser)[3] guay*, (ser) superguay*, (ser) bestial*
great, amazing	(ser)[3] alucinante*
very, hyper	super-, hiper-, ultra-
grotty	cutre*
good-looking	(estar)[3] cachas*
square person	(ser)[3] un/una carca*, (ser) un/una facha*
old fogey, bore	(ser)[3] un/una carroza*, un/una fósil*
parents	los viejos*
my boyfriend	mi chico*
my girlfriend	mi chica*, mi niña*
friend, mate	un/una colega*
police	la pasma*
a bore, a pain	(ser)[3] un/una pelma*, un/una palizas*, un/una plasta*, un/una plomo*, un/una peñazo*, un muermo*
a flirt	(ser)[3] un ligón/una ligona*
stingy person	un/una rata*
skiver	un/una jeta*
thief	un chorizo/una choriza*
knowall	un enterado/una enterada*
nutter	un chalado/una chalada*
money, dough	la tela*, la pasta*
pesetas	las pelas*
1000 ptas note	un talego*
job	un curro*
grub, food	el papeo*
sandwich	un bocata*
clothes	los trapos*
jacket	una chupa*
car	un carro*
cigarette	un cilindro*
a hassle	un lío*
to be a drag	ser un palo*, ser mortal*
to steal, nick	mangar*, birlar*
to work	currar*
to sleep	sobar*
to eat	papear*
to drink	privar*
to like, dig	molar*
not to be interested in	pasar de*
to be cheesed off	estar cabreado/cabreada*
to be low	estar depre*
to be broke	estar a dos velas*
to be lousy	estar chungo/chunga*
to have a bad time	tener un mal rollo*
to blow a fuse	subirse por las paredes*

[1]The plural "s" ending is often dropped in southern Spain. [2]The "d" is dropped in many words ending in "ado". [3]Use with ser or estar (to be) as shown. See page 52.

Spanish pronunciation

To pronounce Spanish well you need the help of a Spanish speaker or language tapes, but these general points will help. Bear in mind that there are exceptions and strong regional variations.

Vowels

a sounds like "a" in "cat".
e sounds like "e" in "let".
i sounds like "i" in "machine".
o sounds like "o" in "soft".
u sounds like "oo" in "moon". It is silent after "q" and usually silent after "g" if it is followed by "e" or "i".

Consonants

c is hard like "c" in "cat" except before "e" or "i" when it is like "th" in thumb.
d is like an English "d" except when it is on the end of a syllable. Then it is like "th" in "that".
g is like the "g" in "good" except before "e" or "i". Then it sounds like "ch" in the Scottish word "loch".
h is never pronounced.
j sounds like "ch" in the Scottish word "loch".
ll sounds like the "y" in "yes" but preceded by a hint of an "l".
ñ sounds like the "ni" sound in "onion".

qu is the same sound as the hard *c* above.
r is a rolled or nearly trilled "r". Double "rr" sounds about the same. At the beginning of a word, "r" is strongly trilled, and on the end of a word it is not trilled quite so much.
v sounds like "b" in "big". There is no difference between a Spanish *b* and a Spanish *v*.
y sounds like "y" in "yes" when it is in the middle of a word. On the end of a word or on its own, e.g. *y* (and), *y* sounds like a Spanish *i* – like the "i" in "machine".

In Spanish you stress the last syllable of most words ending in a consonant. For words ending in a vowel, stress the second-to-last syllable. The stress mark (´ over a vowel), e.g. *día* (day) is used when the general rule does not apply. It shows which syllable should be stressed.

The alphabet in Spanish

Applying the points made above, this is how you say the alphabet: *A, Be, Ce, CHe, De, E, eFe, Ge, Hache, I, Jota, Ka, eLe, eLLe, eMe, eNe, eÑe, O, Pe, Qu, eRre, eSe, Te, U, uVe, W = uve doble, X = equis, Y = i griega, Z = ceta.*

How Spanish works

Nouns

All Spanish nouns are either masculine (m) or feminine (f). Nouns for people and animals have the obvious gender, e.g. *el padre* (father) and *el toro* (bull) are masculine and *la madre* (mother) and *la vaca* (cow) are feminine. For most nouns, though, the gender seems random, e.g. *autobús* (bus) is masculine and *casa* (house) is feminine. A few nouns can be either gender, e.g. *el/la turista* (tourist m/f).

The singular article (the word for "the" or "a") shows the noun's gender:
with (m) nouns, "the" is *el*, e.g. *el autobús* (the bus) and "a" is *un*, e.g. *un autobús* (a bus); with (f) nouns, "the" is *la*, e.g. *la casa* (the house) and "a" is *una*, e.g. *una casa* (a house).

Don't worry if you muddle up *el* and *la*, you will still be understood. It is worth knowing the gender of nouns since other words, particularly adjectives, change to match them. If you're learning a noun, learn it with *el* or *la*. A useful tip is that many nouns ending in "a" are feminine.

Plurals

In the plural, the Spanish for "the" is *los* + masculine noun and *las* + feminine noun, e.g. *los autobuses* (the buses), *las casas* (the houses).
Uno and *una* become *unos* and *unas*, e.g. *unos autobuses* (some buses), *unas casas* (some houses).
To make nouns plural, add "es" to any that end in a consonant, e.g. *un tren, dos trenes* (a train, two trains) and add "s" to most nouns ending in a vowel, e.g. *un billete, dos billetes* (a ticket, two tickets).

A (to) and de (of, from)

In Spanish, "to" is *a*. When *a* precedes *el*, they contract to *al*, e.g. *Voy al mercado* (I'm going to the market).
The Spanish for "of" and "from" is *de*. When *de* precedes *el*, they join up and become *del*, e.g. *Soy del norte* (I'm from the north).
Spanish uses *de* to show possession where English does not, e.g. *el libro de Ana* (Ana's book), *el suéter del niño* (the kid's jumper).

Adjectives

In Spanish most adjectives come after the noun they refer to, e.g. *la película larga* (the long film). They also agree with the noun – they change when used with a feminine or plural noun.

With feminine nouns, adjectives ending in "o" and a few others change to "a", e.g. *corto* becomes *corta*: *la novela corta* (the short novel). Others don't change, e.g. *feliz* (happy). In this book adjectives that change are given twice with the (m) form first, e.g. *corto/corta* (short).

With plural nouns, most adjectives that end in a vowel have an "s", e.g. *rojo* (m) becomes *rojos*: *los trenes rojos* (the red trains), *roja* (f) becomes *rojas*: *las camisetas rojas* (the red T-shirts). Those that end in a consonant have "es", e.g. *difícil* (difficult) becomes *difíciles*: *los exámenes difíciles* (the difficult exams).

Some common adjectives come before the noun, e.g. *gran* (big), *poco/poca* (little).

Making comparisons

To make a comparison, put the following words in front of the adjective:
más (more, ...er), e.g. *más bonita* (prettier);
menos (less), e.g. *menos bonita* (less pretty);
tan (as), e.g. *tan bonita* (as pretty);
el/la más (the most, the ...est), e.g. *la más bonita* (the prettiest);

más ... que(more ... than, ...er ...than), e.g. *El es más alto que ella* (He's taller than her);
menos que (less ... than), e.g. *Ella es menos alta que él* (She's less tall than him);
tan ... como (as ... as), e.g. *El es tan delgado como ella* (He's as thin as her).

There are exceptions, e.g. *bueno/buena* (good), *mejor* (better), *el/la mejor* (the best); *malo/mala* (bad), *peor* (worse), *el/la peor* (the worst).

Very + adjective

Spanish has two ways of saying that something is "very good/easy etc.". You can use *muy* (very) + the adjective, e.g. *muy fácil* (very easy), or the adjective + *-ísimo/ísima*, e.g. *facilísimo/facilísima* (very easy). Vowels on the end of the adjective are dropped, e.g. *caro* (expensive), *carísimo* (very expensive). This second way is used a lot in colloquial Spanish.

Este/esta (this)

The Spanish for "this" is *este* + (m) noun, e.g. *este chico* (this boy), *esta* + (f), e.g. *esta chica* (this girl), *estos* + plural (m) noun, e.g. *estos chicos* (these boys), *estas* + plural (f), e.g. *estas chicas* (these girls).

Ese/esa, aquel/aquella (that)

There are two words for "that": *ese* when the person or thing referred to is near the person you're speaking to, e.g. who's that bloke on your right?, and *aquel* when the person or thing is far from both of you, e.g. that bloke over there.

Ese and *aquel* change as follows: *ese* or *aquel* + (m) noun; *esa* or *aquella* + (f); *esos* or *aquellos* + plural (m) noun; *esas* or *aquellas* + plural (f).

I, you, he, she etc.

Spanish often leaves out "I", "you" etc. The verb changes according to who or what is doing the action (see Verbs, page 52) so they are not needed, e.g. *Estoy pensando* (I am thinking, literally "am thinking"), *Es un bar* (It's a bar, literally "Is a bar"). It helps to know these words as the verb has various forms to correspond to each of them.

I	*yo*
you *tú* or *usted*	There are four words for "you": *tú* is singular informal; say *tú* to a friend or someone your age or younger; *usted*, often written Vd., is singular polite (pol). Use it to a person you don't know or you want to show respect to (someone older);
vosotros/ vosotras or *ustedes*	*vosotros/-as* is plural informal, (m)/(f). Use it like *tú* but when speaking to more than one person. Use *vosotras* when talking to girls or women only; *ustedes* (written Vds.) is plural polite (pl.pol). Use it like *usted* but for more than one person. If in doubt, use the polite forms. Saying *tú* or *vosotros* to people who don't expect it can be rude.
he *él* she *ella* it *(él/ella)*	There's no special word for "it". The verb is used on it's own.
we *nosotros/ nosotras*	*Nosotros* means "we" for males or males and females, *nosotras* means "we" for females only.
they *ellos* or *ellas*	*Ellos* is for males, *ellas* for females.

My, your, his, her etc.

These words agree with the noun they relate to, e.g. *mi hermano* (my brother), *mis padres* (my parents), *nuestra casa* (our house) etc.:

	in front of singular noun	plural noun
my	*mi*	*mis*
your	*tu*	*tus*
his/her/its, your (pol)	*su*	*sus*
our	*nuestro/nuestra*	*nuestros/nuestras*
your	*vuestro/vuestra*	*vuestros/vuestras*
their, your (pl.pol)	*su*	*sus*

Verbs

Spanish verbs have more tenses — present, future, simple past etc. — than English verbs, but there are simple ways of getting by which are explained here.

Present tense

Spanish verbs end in "ar", "er" or "ir" in the infinitive[1], e.g. *comprar* (to buy), *comer* (to eat), *escribir* (to write), and follow one of these three patterns. Drop "ar", "er" or "ir" and replace it with the ending you need:

to buy	*compr ar*		
I buy	*compr o*	we buy	*compr amos*
you buy	*compr as*	you buy	*compr áis*
he/she/it buys, you (pol) buy	*compr a*	they/you (pl.pol) buy	*compr an*

to eat	*com er*		
I eat	*com o*	we eat	*com emos*
you eat	*com es*	you eat	*com éis*
he/she/it eats, you (pol) eat	*com e*	they/you (pl.pol) eat	*com en*

to write	*escrib ir*		
I write	*escrib o*	we write	*escrib imos*
you write	*escrib es*	you write	*escrib ís*
he/she/it writes, you (pol) write	*escrib e*	they/you (pl.pol) write	*escrib en*

Spanish verbs are mostly used without "I", "you" etc. (see I, you, he, she etc. on page 51). It helps to learn them as a list, e.g. *como, comes* etc.

Spanish doesn't distinguish as much as English between present (I write) and present continuous (I'm writing). Unless you want to stress that the action is happening now (e.g. He's sleeping), the present tense is used, e.g. *Viene hoy* (she is coming today, literally "she comes today").

Ser and estar (to be)

Spanish has two verbs "to be". *Ser* is used to describe people and things, e.g. *Soy ingles* (I am English), *Es un camarero* (He's a waiter), and to tell the time, e.g. *Son las tres* (It's three). *Estar* is for saying where people and things are, e.g. *Está lejos* (It's far) and describing anything changeable or short-lived, e.g. *Está de mal humor* (He's in a bad mood). Both are irregular:

to be	*ser*	*estar*
I am	*soy*	*estoy*
you are	*eres*	*estás*
he/she/it is, you (pol) are	*es*	*está*
we are	*somos*	*estamos*
you are	*sois*	*estáis*
they/you (pl.pol) are	*son*	*están*

Other useful irregular verbs

to have (got)	*tener*
I have (got)	*tengo*
you have (got)	*tienes*
he/she/it has (got), you (pol) have (got)	*tiene*
we have (got)	*tenemos*
you have (got)	*tenéis*
they/you (pl.pol) have (got)	*tienen*

	to do	*hacer*	to go	*ir*
I	do	*hago*	go	*voy*
you	do	*haces*	go	*vas*
he/she/it, you (pol)	does	*hace*	goes	*va*
	do		go	
we	do	*hacemos*	go	*vamos*
you	do	*hacéis*	go	*vais*
they, you (pl.pol)	do	*hacen*	go	*van*

to be able to (can)	*poder*		
I can	*puedo*	we can	*podemos*
you can	*puedes*	you can	*podéis*
he/she/it can, you (pol) can	*puede*	they/you (pl.pol) can	*pueden*

Stem-changing verbs

These are verbs whose stem (the part before the infinitive[1] ending) changes as well as the endings. These three are especially useful:

to want	*querer*		
I want	*quiero*	we want	*queremos*
you want	*quieres*	you want	*queréis*
he/she/it wants, you (pol) want	*quiere*	they/you (pl.pol) want	*quieren*

[1]The infinitive is the form in which verbs are given in the Index and in dictionaries. Many Spanish infinitives end in "ar", "er" or "ir". Reflexive verbs end in "se".

to prefer	preferir		
I prefer	prefiero	we prefer	preferimos
you prefer	prefieres	you prefer	preferís
he/she/it prefiere		they/you	prefieren
you (pol) prefer(s)		(pl.pol) prefer	

to play	jugar		
I play	juego	we play	jugamos
you play	juegas	you play	jugáis
he/she/it juega		they/you	juegan
plays, you (pol) play		(pl.pol) play	

Reflexive verbs

Spanish has far more reflexive verbs than English. They all have "se" infinitive[1] endings, e.g. *lavarse* (to get washed/wash oneself), *levantarse* (to get up, literally "to get oneself up"). Here is the present of a common one:

I get up	me levanto
you get up	te levantas
he/she/you (pol) gets up	se levanta
we get up	nos levantamos
you get up	os levantáis
they/you (pl.pol) get up	se levantan

Talking about the future

"Ar", "er" and "ir" verbs (see Present tense) all have the same endings in the future tense:

I shall buy	comprar é
you will buy	comprar ás
he/she/it will buy	comprar á
you (pol) will buy	
we shall buy	comprar emos
you will buy	comprar éis
they/you (pl.pol) will buy	comprar án

Another future tense is made with the present of *ir* (to go) + *a* + the verb's infinitive, e.g. *Voy a comprar* (I'm going to buy). It is used for something that is just about to happen.

Talking about the past

The most useful past tense in Spanish is the simple past tense. "Ar" verbs have one set of endings and "er" and "ir" verbs have another:

to buy	compr ar		
I bought	compr é	we bought	compr amos
you bought	compr aste	you bought	compr asteis
he/she/it	compr ó	they/you	compr aron
you (pol) bought		(pl.pol) bought	

to eat	com er		
I ate	com í	we ate	com imos
you ate	com iste	you ate	com isteis
he/she/it com io		they/you	com ieron
you (pol) ate		(pl.pol) ate	

The past tenses of "to be" and "to do" are also useful:

to be		ser	estar
I was		fui	estuve
you were		fuiste	estuviste
he/she/it was		fue	estuvo
you (pl.pol) were			
we were		fuimos	estuvimos
you were		fuisteis	estuvisteis
they/you (pl.pol) were	fueron		estuvieron

The past tense of *ir* (to go) is the same as the past tense of *ser*, so *fui* can also mean "I went", *fue* (he/she/it went), *fuimos* (we went) etc.

to do	hacer		
I did	hice	we did	hicimos
you did	hiciste	you did	hicisteis
he/she/it	hizo	they/you	hicieron
you (pol) did		(pl.pol) did	

Negatives

To make a sentence negative put *no* in front of the verb, e.g. *No comprendo* (I don't understand), *No me levanto* (I don't get up).

Other useful negative words include *nunca* (never), *nadie* (nobody), *nada* (nothing), *ninguno/ninguna* (any).

Making questions

To make a question, just give a sentence the intonation of a question – raise your voice at the end. In written Spanish you put an upside down question mark at the start and a standard one at the end, e.g. *¿Quieres comer?* (Do you want to eat?).

Questions can begin with words like:

who?	¿quién?
what?	¿qué?
when?	¿cuándo?
how?	¿cómo?
where?	¿dónde?
how much?	¿cuánto/cuánta?
which? what?	¿cuál?

Exclamations

In written Spanish you put an upside down exclamation mark at the start and a standard one at the end, e.g. *¡Claro!* (Of course!)

Numbers, colours, countries etc.

Numbers

0	cero	15	quince	80	ochenta
1	uno[1]/una	16	dieciséis	81	ochenta y uno
2	dos	17	diecisiete	90	noventa
3	tres	18	dieciocho	91	noventa y uno
4	cuatro	19	diecinueve	100	cien, ciento[2]
5	cinco	20	veinte	101	ciento uno
6	seis	21	veintiuno	200	doscientos/doscientas
7	siete	22	veintidós	300	trescientos/trescientas
8	ocho	30	treinta	1,000	mil
9	nueve	31	treinta y uno	2,000	dos mil
10	diez	40	cuarenta	10,000	diez mil
11	once	50	cincuenta	100,000	cien mil
12	doce	60	sesenta	1,000,000	un millón
13	trece	70	setenta	2,000,000	dos millones
14	catorce	71	setenta y uno		

Colours

colour	color
light	claro
dark	oscuro
black	negro/negra
blue	azul
navy	azul marino
brown	marrón
green	verde
grey	gris
orange	naranja
pink	rosa
purple	morado/morada
red	rojo/roja
white	blanco/blanca
yellow	amarillo/amarilla

Days and dates

Monday	lunes	April	abril
Tuesday	martes	May	mayo
Wednesday	miércoles	June	junio
Thursday	jueves	July	julio
Friday	viernes	August	agosto
Saturday	sábado	September	setiembre,
Sunday	domingo		septiembre
January	enero	October	octubre
February	febrero	November	noviembre
March	marzo	December	diciembre

day	el día
week	la semana
month	el mes
year	el año
a diary	una agenda
a calendar	un calendario
yesterday	ayer
the day before yesterday	anteayer
today	hoy
tomorrow	mañana
the day after tomorrow	pasado mañana
the next day	el próximo día
last week	la semana pasada
this week	esta semana
next week	la semana próxima

What day is it today?	¿Qué día es hoy?
What's the date?	¿Qué fecha es?
on Monday	el lunes
on Mondays	los lunes
in August	en agosto
1st April	el primero/uno de abril
23rd November	el veintitrés de noviembre
9th September	el nueve de setiembre

1990	mil novecientos noventa
1991	mil novecientos noventa y uno
1999	mil novecientos noventa y nueve

Seasons

season	la estación, la temporada
spring	la primavera
summer	el verano
autumn	el otoño
winter	el invierno

Time

hour	hora
minute	minuto
morning (6 am-noon)	la mañana
in the morning	por la mañana
afternoon (12 pm-7 pm)	la tarde
in the afternoon	por la tarde
evening (7 pm-midnight),	la noche
night	la noche
at night	por la noche
morning (midnight-6 am)	la madrugada
midday	el mediodía
midnight	la medianoche

What time is it?	¿Qué hora es?
It's 1 o'clock.	Es la una en punto.
It's 2 o'clock.	Son las dos en punto.

1 o'clock	la una
2 o'clock	las dos
a quarter past two	los dos y cuarto
half past two	las dos y media
a quarter to two	las dos menos cuarto
five past three	las tres y cinco
ten to four	las cuatro menos diez

What time...?	¿A qué hora...?
in ten minutes	dentro de diez minutos
half an hour ago	hace media hora
at 09 00	a las nueve
at 13.17	a las trece diecisiete

[1] Uno drops the "o" before masculine nouns, e.g. un libro (one book). [2] Cien changes into ciento when followed by a smaller number.

Weather

What's the weather like?	¿Qué tiempo hace?
What's the weather forecast?	¿Cuál es el pronóstico del tiempo?
It's fine.	Hace buen tiempo.
It's sunny.	Hace sol.
It's hot.	Hace calor.
It's horrible.	Hace un tiempo horrible.
It's cold.	Hace frío.
It's windy.	Hace viento.
It's raining.	Está lloviendo.
It's snowing.	Está nevando.
It's foggy.	Hay niebla.
It's icy.	Hay hielo./Hace muchísimo frío.
sky	el cielo
sun	el sol
clouds	las nubes
rain	la lluvia
umbrella	el paraguas
waterproof	el impermeable

Nationalities

The easiest way to say where you come from is to say Soy de (I am from) + name of country, e.g.:

I am from Spain.	Soy de España.
Are you from Wales?	¿Eres de Gales?

I am not from England.	No soy de Inglaterra.
She is from Scotland.	Es de Escocia.

You can also say Soy (I am) + adjective for nationality, e.g. Soy español/española (I am Spanish). Here are some common adjectives:

American	americano/americana
Australian	australiano/australiana
Canadian	canadiense
English	inglés/inglesa
French	francés/francesa
Irish	irlandés/irlandesa
Portuguese	portugués/portuguesa
Scottish	escocés/escocesa
Spanish	español/española
Welsh	galés/galesa

Faiths and beliefs

I'm...	Soy...
an agnostic	un agnóstico/una agnóstica
an atheist	un ateo/una atea
Buddhist	budista
Catholic	católico/católica
Christian	cristiano/cristiana
Hindu	hindú
Jewish	judío/judía
Muslim	musulmán/musulmana
Protestant	protestante
Sikh	sikh, sig

Countries and continents

world	el mundo	China	China	North Africa	Africa del Norte
continent	el continente	Dominica	Dominica	Pakistan	Pakistán
country	el país	England	Inglaterra	Poland	Polonia
border	la frontera	Europe	Europa	Portugal	Portugal
ocean	el océano	France	Francia	Russia	Rusia
sea	el mar	Germany	Alemania	Scandinavia	Escandinavia
north	el norte	Great Britain	Gran Bretaña	Scotland	Escocia
south	el sur	Greece	Grecia	South America	América del Sur/Sudamérica
east	el este	Grenada	Granada		
west	el oeste	Hungary	Hungría	Spain	España
		India	India	Switzerland	Suiza
Africa	Africa	Ireland	Irlanda	Trinidad	Trinidad
Algeria	Argelia	Israel	Israel	Tunisia	Túnez
Asia	Asia	Italy	Italia	Turkey	Turquía
Australia	Australia	Jamaica	Jamaica	Uganda	Uganda
Austria	Austria	Japan	Japón	United States	Estados Unidos, USA
Bangladesh	Bangladesh	Kenya	Kenia		
Barbados	Barbados	Latin America	América Latina	USSR	URSS
Belgium	Bélgica	Mexico	Méjico	Vietnam	Vietnam
Canada	Canadá	Middle East	Oriente Medio	Wales	Gales
Caribbean	El Caribe	Morocco	Marruecos	West Indies	Antillas
Central America	Centroamérica	Netherlands	Holanda		
		New Zealand	Nueva Zelanda		

Index

This Index lists the most essential words. If you can't find the word you want, look up a relevant entry, e.g. to find "garlic" look under "vegetables". Adjectives with two forms are given twice: (m) followed by (f) (see page 51), and verbs are in the infinitive (see page 52).

to buy, 6	comprar	coffee, 16	el café
bye, 3	adiós, hasta la vista	black	el café solo
		white	el café con leche
café, 16-17	el café	coke, 16	la coca-cola
cake	el pastel	cold, 11, 13	frío/fría
(telephone) call, 13	la llamada	a cold, 46	un resfriado
to call, to call back 13,15	llamar	to collect, 44	coleccionar
		college, 42	la escuela
calm, 8	liso, en calma	types of, 43	
to camp, 10	acampar	colour, 24, 26, 54	color
camping, 10-11	el camping	to come, 37	venir
campsites, 10	campings	a comic, 33	un comic
to cancel, 8	cancelar	commercial, 33	comercial
can opener, 11	el abrelatas	compact disc, 28	el compact disc
car, 9	el coche	completely, 36	completamente
parts of, 9		computer, 44	la computadora
caravan, 11	la caravana	concert, 29	el concierto
career, 45	carrera	to confirm, 8	confirmar
car park, 5	el aparcamiento	constipated, 46	estreñimiento
carrier bag, 25	la bolsa	contact lens, 47	la lente de contacto
to carry	llevar, seguir	cool, 27, 37	chulo/chula
to carry on, 4	seguir	corner, 5	la esquina
cashier's desk, 15	la caja	to cost, 5	costar
cassette, 28	el casete	Could I have..., 3	Quisiera...
castle, 30	el castillo	countries, 55	
casualty department, 47	emergencias	countryside, 30	el campo
		cramp, 46	la rampa
to catch, 39	coger	crash helmet, 9	el casco
cathedral, 30	la catedral	crazy, 37	loco/loca
to cause trouble, 47	molestar	credit card, 15	la tarjeta de crédito
caves, 30	las cuevas	a creep, 37	un pelotillero/una pelotillera
chair, 16	la silla		
to change, 6, 8	cambiar	crisps, 25	las patatas fritas, las papas
changing room, 27	el probador		
channel (TV), 33	el canal	to cross, 4	cruzar
charter flight, 8	el vuelo charter	crossroads, junction, 4	el cruce de carreteras
cheap, 11	barato/barata	curly, 36	rizado
cheaper, cheapest, 24	más barato/barata	currency, 15	moneda
		currents, 40	las corrientes
to cheat, 39	hacer trampas	customs, 8	la aduana
to check in, 8	presentarse	to cut, 46	cortar
check-out, 22	la caja	to cut oneself	cortarse
Cheers!, 16	¡Salud!	cut price, 8	de precio reducido
cheese, 16, 18	el queso		
chemist, 22, 46	la farmacia	to dance, 30, 36	bailar
chicken, 21	el pollo	danger, 47	peligro
chips, 18	las patatas fritas	dangerous, 40	peligroso/peligrosa
chocolate, 25	el chocolate	dark (colouring), 36	moreno/morena
church, 5, 30	la iglesia	dates, 54	fechas
cigarette	el cigarrillo	day, 54	el día
cinema, 5, 30, 33	el cine	day after tomorrow, 30, 54	pasado mañana
clean, 11	limpio/limpia		
clever, 36	listo/lista	dead end, 5	calle sin salida
close, 5	cerca	delay, 8	el retraso
closed, 22	cerrado/cerrada	delicious, 21	muy bueno/buena
clothes, 26-27	la ropa	demo, 45	la marcha, la manifestación
club, 30	el club nocturno, la disco		
		dentist, 46	el/la dentista
club (sports), 39	el club	deodorant, 12	el desodorante
coach (bus), 7	el autobús	department store, 22	los grandes almacenes
coast, 30	la costa	departure gate, 8	la puerta de salida
(telephone) code, 14	el prefijo	departures, 7	salidas

depressed, 37 — *deprimido/deprimida*
dessert, 18 — *el postre*
diarrhoea, 46 — *diarrea*
dictionary, 46 — *el diccionario*
difficult, 44 — *difícil*
dinner, 11, 21 — *la cena*
(film) director, 33 — *el director*
(telephone) directory, 15 — *el listín telefónico, la guía de teléfonos*
discipline, 43 — *la disciplina*
disco, 30 — *la discoteca*
divorced, 35 — *divorciado/divorciada*
dizzy, 46 — *mareado/mareada*
to do, 34, 52 — *hacer*
to do (study), 42, 43 — *estudiar*
doctor, 46 — *el doctor, el médico/ la doctora, la médica*

(car) documents, 9 — *los papeles*
doubles, 39 — *dobles*
doughnut, 16 — *churro*
downstairs, 13 — *abajo*
to draw (sports), 39 — *empatar*
to draw, 4 — *dibujar*
(salad) dressing, 18 — *la vinagreta*
dressy, 27 — *bien vestido/vestida*
drink, 17 — *la bebida*
  types of, 16-17
to drink, 11, 16 — *beber*
to go for a drink, 30 — *ir de copas*
drinking water, 11, 47 — *agua potable*
not drinking water, 47 — *agua no potable*
to drive — *conducir*
driving licence, 9 — *el carnet de conducir*
drugs, 45 — *las drogas*
to dry, 12 — *secar*
dubbed, 33 — *doblado/doblada*
dull, boring, 30 — *aburrido/aburrida*

easy, 44 — *fácil*
easy going, 43 — *tranquilo/tranquila*
to eat, 16 — *comer*
eating, 16-17, 18-19, 20-21
eggs, 21 — *los huevos*
electric socket, 13 — *el enchufe*
emergencies, 47 — *emergencias*
emergency exit, 47 — *salida de emergencia*
end of, at the end, 5 — *al final*
engine, 9 — *el motor*
English, 3, 55 — *inglés*
enough, 21, 25, 41 — *suficiente*
enquiries, 15 — *información*
entertainment guide — *la cartelera*
entrance, 22 — *la entrada*
environment, 45 — *el medio ambiente*
evening, 13, 30, 54 — *la noche*
every day, 7 — *diario/diaria*
exams, 43 — *los exámenes*
except, 7 — *excepto*
exchange (holiday), 35 — *el intercambio*
exchange rate, 15 — *la tarifa de cambio*

exciting, 33 — *emocionante*
excuse me, 3, 19 — *perdone/perdona, por favor*
exhibition, 30 — *la exposición*
exit, 22 — *la salida*
to expect, 15 — *esperar*
expelled — *expulsado/expulsada*
expensive, 11, 41 — *caro/cara*
to explain, 45 — *explicar*
extra — *extra*
eyes, 36 — *los ojos*

fair (colouring), 36 — *rubio/rubia*
family, 35 — *la familia*
fan (music), 29 — *el/la fan*
far, 5 — *lejos*
fare, 7 — *el precio, la tarifa*
fashion, 27 — *la moda*
fashionable, 27 — *de moda*
fat, 36 — *gordo/gorda*
father, 35 — *el padre*
to be fed up, 48 — *estar harto/harta*
feminist, 45 — *el/la feminista*
ferry, 8 — *el barco*
film (camera), 24 — *la película*
film (cinema), 31, 32-33 — *la película*
film buff, 33 — *el experto en cine*
film showing, 30 — *la sesión*
to finish, 30, 42 — *terminar*
Fire!, 47 — *¡Fuego!*
fire brigade, 47 — *los bomberos*
fireworks, 30 — *los fuegos artificiales*
first — *primero/primera*
fish, 18, 21 — *el pescado*
to fix, 9 — *reparar*
flat (apartment), 35 — *el piso*
flea market, 22 — *el rastro*
flight, 8 — *vuelo*
flight number, 8 — *el número de vuelo*
floor, 13 — *el suelo*
flu, 46 — *la gripe*
to follow, 4, 47 — *seguir*
food, 16, 18-19, 21, 23, 25 — *la comida*
food poisoning, 46 — *la intoxicación*
foreign exchange, 15 — *cambio extranjero*
foreign exchange office, 15 — *cambio*
fork, 21 — *el tenedor*
fountain, 31 — *la fuente*
free (empty), 16 — *vacío/vacía*
free (school), 43 — *gratis*
friend, 36 — *el amigo/la amiga*
fruit, 18, 25 — *la fruta*
fruit juice, 16 — *el zumo de fruta*
fruit/veg stall, 22 — *la verdulería*
full, 10 — *completo/completa*
fun, funny, 33 — *divertido/divertida*
the future, 45 — *el futuro*

game, 38, 39 — *la partida*

games, 44	juegos
garage, 9	el taller
garlic, 21	el ajo
gay, 45	gay
gears, 9	las marchas
(hair) gel, 24	le gel fijador
gig, 29	el concierto
girl, 36	la chica
girlfriend, 35	la novia
glass, 16	el vaso
glasses, 47	las gafas
to go, 4, 52	ir
to go out with, 37	salir con
a goal, 39	el gol
god, 45	dios
goggles, 40	las gafas de natación
good, 33, 43	bueno/buena
goodbye, 3, 13	adiós
good-looking, 36	está bueno/buena
not good-looking, 36	no es guapo/guapa
in a good mood, 37	de buen humor
gossip, 36-37	cotilleo
grant (student), 43	la beca
greengrocer, 22	la verdulería
greetings, 3, 12	
group (musicians), 29	el grupo
guide book, 30	la guía
hair, 36	el pelo
hairdryer, 12	el secador
ham, 16	jamón
hamburger, 18	la hamburguesa
handbag, 47	bolso
hand luggage, 8	el equipaje de mano
hang on, 15	un momento
hangover, 46	la resaca
happy, 37	feliz
hassled, 37	enfadado/enfadada
to have, 52	tener
hayfever, 46	fiebre del heno
headache, 46	dolor de cabeza
headphones, 28	los auriculares
health food shop, 22	la tienda naturista, la herboristería
to hear, 29	oír
heavy, 8	pesado/pesada
hello, 3, 12	hola
Help!, 47	¡Ayuda!
to help, 4, 20	ayudar
here, 5, 34	aquí
Hi!, 3	¡Hola!
hi-fi, 28	la cadena de alta fidelidad
to hire, 9	alquilar
bikes and mopeds, 9	
skis, 41	
hit (music), 29	el éxito
to hitch, 9	hacer autostop
holiday, 35, 43	las vacaciones
homework, 43	los deberes
horrible, 36	horrible
hospital, 47	el hospital

hot, 11	calor/caliente
(too) hot, spicy, 21	(demasiado) picante
hot chocolate, 16	el chocolate caliente
hotel, 10	el hotel
house, 35	la casa
How?, 3	¿Cómo?
How are you?, 12	¿Cómo está?/¿Cómo estás?
How long? (time), 34	¿Cuánto tiempo?
How many?, 3	¿Cuántos?/¿Cuántas?
How much?, 3	¿Cuánto?/¿Cuánta?
How much is it?, 3, 22	¿Cuánto cuesta?, ¿Cuánto cuesta esto?
How often?, 38	¿Cada cuándo?
hungry, 21	hambre
to hurt a little, 46	doler un poco
to hurt a lot, 46	doler mucho
husband, 35	el marido
ice, 16	el hielo
ice-cream, 16	el helado
ID, 47	papeles
idea, 30	la idea
idiot, 37	el/la idiota
I'd like..., 3	Quisiera/quiero...
important, 45	importante
ill	enfermo/enferma
illness, 46-47	enfermedad
I'm in trouble., 47	Tengo problemas.
I'm lost., 47	Me he perdido.
in, 5	en, dentro
indoor, 39	cubierta
infection, 46	la infección
information, 8	información
in front of, 5	delante de
injection, 46	la inyección
(musical) instrument, 29	el instrumento
insurance, 9, 47	el seguro
interesting, 30	interesante
interests, 45	intereses
Is there...?, 3	¿Hay...?
It/this is..., 3	Es/esto es...
jacket, 27	la chaqueta
jam, 21	la mermelada
jealous, 37	celoso/celosa
jeans, 26	los tejanos
job, 45	el trabajo
journey, 6	el trayecto
junction, crossroads, 4	el cruce de carreteras
Keep out!, 47	¡Prohibido el paso!
ketchup, 18	salsa de tomate
key, 11, 13, 47	la llave
kind (type), 28	tipo
to kiss, 37	besar
knife, 21	el cuchillo
to know, 3, 36	saber, conocer
laid-back, 37	tranquilo/tranquila
lake, 30	el lago

languages, 42	los idiomas
large	grande
last, 7	último/última
later, 45	después
latest, 7	último/última
launderette, 22	la lavandería
to lay the table, 20	poner la mesa
lazy, 37	vago/vaga
to learn, 29	aprender
to leave (depart), 7	salir
to leave (a message), 15	dejar
lecture, 43	la clase
lecturer, 43	el profesor/la profesora
left, 4	izquierda
left luggage locker, 7	la consigna automática
lemon, 16	el limón
a slice of, 16	una rodaja de
less, 25	menos
lesson (school), 43	la clase
lesson (sports), 41	la lección
letter, 15	la carta
library, 33	la biblioteca
lifeguard, 47	el socorrista
to like	gustar
to like, want, 3, 31, 52	querer
to listen, 28	escuchar
litre, 9	el litro
a little, 20	un poco
live (music), 29	música en directo
to live, 34, 35	vivir
to live with, 35	vivir con
liver, 21	el hígado
loads, 42	cantidad
a loan, 43	el préstamo
long, 27, 36	largo/larga
loo, 12	el lavabo/los servicios
loo paper, 11	el papel higiénico
look (style), 27	el estilo
to look, 24	mirar
to look for, 10	buscar
to lose, 14, 39	perder
lost, 4	perdido
lost property, 47	objetos perdidos
loud, 28	alto/alta
loudspeaker, 7	el altavoz
lousy, 33	malísimo/malísima
to love, 40	encantar
luggage, 8	equipaje
lunch, 11	la comida
machine, 6	la máquina
macho, 37	machista
mad, 37	loco/loca
Madam, Mrs, 3, 12	señora
main	principal
main course, 18	el segundo plato
make-up, 24	el maquillaje
man	el hombre
map, 4, 5	el mapa

march, demo, 45	la marcha, la manifestación
margarine, 21	la margarina
market, 22	el mercado
married, 35	casado/casada
mask, 40	las gafas de submarinismo
match (sports), 39	el partido
a box of matches, 11	la caja de cerillas
mate, 36	el tío/la tía
maybe, 3	quizás
mayonnaise, 18	la mayonesa
meal, 21	la comida
to mean, 3	significar
meat, 18, 21	la carne
medicines, 46	los medicamentos
medium, 27	mediano/mediana
to meet, 8, 31	encontrarse
menu, 16, 19	el menú
message, 15	el recado
milk, 16	la leche
milkshake, 16	el batido
mineral water, 16	el agua mineral
fizzy	con gas
still	sin gas
Miss, 3	señorita
mixed up, 37	no aclararse
money, 14, 15, 47	el dinero
month, 54	el mes
mood, 37	humor
moped, 9	la motocicleta
more, 25	más
morning, 30, 54	la mañana
mosquito bites, 46	las picaduras de mosquito
mother, 35	la madre
motorbike, 9	la moto
motorway, 5	la autopista
mountains, 30	la montaña
movie, 33	la película
Mr, Sir, 3, 12	señor
Mrs, 3, 12	señora
museum, 5, 30	el museo
music, 28-29	la música
music/pop video, 28	el video musical, el video-pop
mustard, 18	la mostaza
My name is..., 35	Me llamo...
nasty, 36	horrible
nationalities, 55	
national service, 43	el servicio militar, la mili
near, 5	cerca
nearby, 5	cerca de aquí
new, 29	nuevo/nueva
news, 33	las noticias
newspapers, 24	los periódicos
next, 6, 7	próximo/próxima
next to, 5	al lado de
nice (OK), 36	simpático/simpática
nickname, 35	el apodo

night, 11	la noche	to pay, 11, 13	pagar
nightclub, 30	el club nocturno, la disco	peace, 45	la paz
no, 3	no	peanuts, 25	los cacahuetes
no entry, 5, 47	dirección prohibida, prohibido el paso	pedestrian crossing, 4	el paso para peatones
		pedestrians, 5	los peatones
no-one, 53	nadie	pen, ballpoint, 24	el bolígrafo
no parking, 5	prohibido aparcar	people, 10	la gente
no smoking	prohibido fumar	pepper, 18	la pimienta
no swimming, 47	prohibido el baño	performance (film), 30	la sesión
not at all, 3	de nada	period, 46	el periodo, la regla
novel, 33	la novela	personal stereo, 28	el stereo personal
now, nowadays, 45	ahora	petrol, 9	la gasolina
nuclear disarmament, 45	el desarmamento nuclear	petrol station, 9	la gasolinera
		phone, 13, 14-15	teléfono
nuclear power, 45	la energía nuclear	phone box, 13	la cabina
number, 15	el número	phone number, 15	el número de teléfono
number one (record), 29	el número uno	photography, 33, 44	la fotografía
		picnic, 30	el picnic, la excursión
numbers, 3, 54		pill, 46	la pastilla
		pizza, 18	la pizza
offbeat, 33	original	plants, 45	las plantas
oil, 9	el aceite	plate, 21	el plato
OK, 36	simpático/simpática, bien	platform, 7	el andén
		play (theatre), 33	la obra de teatro
OK (looks), 36	está bien	to play, 29, 38	jugar
OK (nice), 36	simpático/simpática	please, 3	por favor
old	viejo/vieja	pocket money, 44	dinero de bolsillo
old-fashioned, 36	anticuado/anticuada	poetry, 33	la poesía
the old town, 30	el centro histórico	police, 47	la policía
omelette, 16	la tortilla	police station, 47	la comisaría de policía
on, 5	en, encima	politics, 45	la política
one way, 5	dirección única	pollution, 45	la polución
open, 22	abierto/abierta	poor, 45	pobre
opposite, 5	en frente de	pork, 21	la carne de cerdo
optician, 46	el/la oculista, el óptico/la óptica	port, 8	el puerto
		postbox, 15	el buzón
		postcard, 15, 24	la postal
or, 3	o	poste restante, 15	lista de correos
orange juice, 16	el zumo de naranja	post office, 5	la oficina de correos, correos
to order, 18	pedir		
other	otro/otra	power (electricity), 47	la corriente eléctrica
other time, 37	otro día	to prefer, 40	preferir
outdoor, 39	al aire libre	pregnant	encinta
out-of-date, 27	pasado de moda	pretty, 36	guapa
over, 5	sobre	price, 18, 22	el precio
over the top, 33	exagerado/exagerada	private property, 47	propiedad privada
		problems, 47	
pal, 36	el tío/la tía	programme (TV), 33	el programa
papers (personal), 47	los papeles	puncture, 9	el pinchazo
parcel, 15	el paquete	to put	poner
parents, 35	los padres	to put down	dejar
park, 5	el parque		
parking meters, 5	los parquímetros	qualifications, 45	las calificaciones necesarias
part-time job, 44	el trabajo de jornada reducida		
		Quick!, 39	¡Rápido!
party, 30	la fiesta	quite, 37	bastante
to pass, 20	pasar		
passport, 8, 47	el pasaporte	racket, 38	la raqueta
the past, 45	el pasado	(car) radiator, 9	el radiador
pasta, 21	la pasta	radio, 28	la radio
path, footpath, 5	la senda, el camino	radio-cassette player, 28	el radio-casete
pavement, 5	la calzada		

railway line, 5	la vía del tren
(Spanish) railways, 7	Renfe
railway station, 7	la estación de tren
rain, 55	la lluvia
raw, 21	crudo/cruda
to read, 32	leer
really, 36	realmente
record player, 28	el tocadiscos
records, 28	los discos
record shop, 28	la tienda de discos
reduction, 7	el descuento
region, 30	la región
(by) registered post, 15	la carta certificada
religion, 45, 55	la religión
to repair, 23	arreglar
replacement, 14	repuesto
to reserve, 7	reservar
restaurant, 11, 18-19	el restaurante
reverse charge call, 15	la llamada a cobro revertido
rice, 21	el arroz
rich, well-off, 45	rico/rica
right, 4	derecha
to be right 45	tener razón
right on, 36	está al día
ringroad, 5	la carretera de circunvalación
river, 5, 30	el río
road, 4	la carretera
room, 10, 11	la habitación
rough, 8	bravo, picado
roundabout, 4	el cruce giratorio
rucksack, backpack, 8	la mochila
rude, 37	mal educado/educada
rules, 39	las reglas
to run	correr
sad, 33	triste
safety pin, 27	el imperdible
salad, 18	la ensalada
sale, 27	las rebajas
salt, 18	la sal
salty, 21	salado/salada
sandwich, 16	el sandwich
satellite TV, 33	la televisión satélite
satirical, 33	satírico/satírica
sausages, 18	las salchichas
to say	decir
to say again, repeat, 3	repetir
scary, 33	de miedo
school, 5, 33, 42	el colegio, la escuela
types of, 43	
scissors, 13	las tijeras
the score (sports), 38	el tanteo
scruffy, 27	desastrado/ desastrada
sea, 40	el mar
sea sick, 8	mareado/mareada
seat, 7	el asiento
second, 4	segundo/segunda
second-hand	de segunda mano
section, 28	la sección

to see, 11	ver
to see again, 37	ver otra vez
see you...	
later, 3	hasta luego
soon, 3	hasta pronto
selfish, 37	egoísta
to sell, 23	vender
serious, 33	serio/seria
sex, 33	sexo
shade, 40	la sombra
shampoo, 12	el champú
shopping centre, 22	el centro comercial
shops, 5, 11, 22-23, 24-25	las tiendas
short, 27, 36	corto/corta, bajo/baja
show (entertainment), 30	el espectáculo
to show, 5	indicar
shower (bathroom), 12	la ducha
Shut up!, 48	¡Cállate!
shy, 37	tímido/tímida
to be sick, 46	vomitar
sightseeing, 30	visitas turísticas
silly, 33	tonto/tonta
to sing, 29	cantar
single (record), 28	el single, el sencillo
single (unmarried), 35	soltero/soltera
singles, 39	individuales
Sir, Mr, 3, 12	señor
sister, 35	la hermana
size, 26, 27	la talla
skiing, 41	el esquí
to skive, 43	hacer novillos, hacer campana
to sleep, 12	dormir
sleeping bag, 13	el saco de dormir
a slice of, 25	la tajada
sloaney, 37	pijo/pija
slower, 3	más despacio
small, 25	pequeño/pequeña
small change, 15	la calderilla
smaller, 24, 27	más pequeño/ pequeña
smart, 27	elegante
to smoke, 47	fumar
snack, 16	la tapa
snow, 41	la nieve
so, 36	tan
soap, 12	el jabón
soap (opera), 33	el serial
socket, 47	el enchufe
someone, 36	alguien
something, 32	algo
song, 28	la canción
sore throat, 46	dolor de garganta
sorry, 3	perdone/perdona
soup, 18	la sopa
spaghetti, 18	los espaguetis
Spanish, 3, 55	español
spare time, 44	tiempo libre
to speak, 3	hablar
special offer, 8	oferta especial

(too) spicy, 21	(demasiado) picante	table, 16	la mesa
to split, to split up, 26, 27	romper	to take, 4	tomar
		take-away, 18	para llevar
spoon, 21	la cuchara	tall, 36	alto/alta
sport, 38-39, 40-41	el deporte	tape, 28	el casete
sports centre, 39	el centro de deportes	to tape, 28	grabar
square, 5	la plaza	tap water, 11	el agua del grifo
square (old-fashioned), 36	anticuado/anticuada	taxi, 8	el taxi
stadium, 39	el estadio	tea, 16	
stairs, 22	la escalera	with lemon	el té con limón
stamp, 15	el sello	with milk	el té con leche
standby, 8	aviso	teacher, 43	el maestro/la maestra
to start, 30	empezar	team, 39	el equipo
starter, 18	el primer plato	telephone, 13, 14-15	teléfono
(radio) station, 28	la emisora	telephone box, 15	la cabina de teléfono
(railway) station, 7	la estación	to tell, 15	decir
to stay, 35	estar	telly, TV, 33	la tele
steak, 18	el bistec	a temperature, 46	fiebre
medium	poco hecho	tent, 11	la tienda
rare	muy poco hecho	term, 42	el trimestre
well done	muy hecho	beginning of, 43	el principio del trimestre
to steal, 47	robar		
to sting, 46	picar	thank you, 3	gracias
stomach ache, 46	dolor de estómago	theatre, 33	el teatro
straight (hair), 36	lacio	there, 5	allí
straight ahead, 4	todo recto	there is, 3	hay
street, 4	la calle	thick, 36	burro/burra
strict, 43	estricto/estricta	thin, 36	delgado/delgada
strong, 40	fuerte	things, 12, 47	cosas
stuck up, 37	pretencioso/ prentenciosa	to think, 32, 45	pensar
		to think about, 24	pensar, pensarlo
student, 42	el/la estudiante	third, 4	tercero/tercera
student fare, 7	la tarifa de estudiante	Third World, 45	el Tercer Mundo
student ticket, 30	la entrada de estudiante	thirsty, 21	sed
		to throw, 39	tirar
to study, 35	estudiar	ticket, 6, 7, 8, 30	el billete, la entrada
style, 27	el estilo	ticket office, 7, 30	la taquilla de billetes/ la ventanilla
subjects, 42, 43	las asignaturas		
with subtitles, 33	con subtítulos	tight, 27	ceñido/ceñida
suburbs, 5	las afueras	till, 15	la caja
subway, 4	el paso subterráneo	time, 54	tiempo, la hora
sugar, 16	el azúcar	timetable, 7	el horario
suitcase, 8	la maleta	tired, 13	cansado/cansada
sun, 40	el sol	tissues, 24	los pañuelos de papel
sunbathing, 40	tomar el sol	today, 30, 54	hoy
sunglasses, 23	gafas de sol	toilet, 12	el lavabo, los servicios
sunscreen, 24	la crema con protección total	toilet paper, 11	el papel higiénico
		toilet, public, 4	los lavabos públicos
sunstroke, 46	la insolación	gents (sign)	caballeros
sun-tan lotion, 24	la crema bronceadora	ladies (sign)	damas
supermarket, 22	el super, el supermercado	toll, 9	el peaje
		tomorrow, 30, 54	mañana
to support (sports), 45	ser partidario/a	tonight, 30, 54	esta noche
surfboard, 40	la plancha de surf	too, 21, 37	demasiado, también
surname, 35	apellido	toothache, 46	dolor de muelas
sweet (taste), 21	dulce	toothpaste, 12	el dentrífico
sweets, 25	los dulces	the Top 40, 29	los cuarenta principales
to swim, 11, 40	nadar		
swimming pool, 11	la piscina	tour (music), 29	la gira
swimsuit, trunks, 27	el bañador	tour (sightseeing), 30	la excursión
		tourist office, 5, 10, 31	Oficina de Información y Turismo

First published in 1990 by Usborne Publishing Ltd.
Usborne House, 83-85 Saffron Hill
London EC1N 8RT, England
Copyright © 1990 Usborne Publishing Ltd.